You begin where I end

SARANG JAIRAJ

Srishti
PUBLISHERS & DISTRIBUTORS

Srishti Publishers & Distributors
Registered Office: N-16, C.R. Park
New Delhi – 110 019
Corporate Office: 212A, Peacock Lane
Shahpur Jat, New Delhi – 110 049
editorial@srishtipublishers.com

First published by
Srishti Publishers & Distributors in 2019

10 9 8 7 6 5 4 3 2 1

Printed and bound in India

You begin where I end

Dedicated to me.

(Because I worked really hard for this book, duh!)

And honestly I don't really have anything to say
I'm goin' through a dilemma, now I'm feeling kinda faint
Got too many things that's happening, goin' on in my brain
And now I'm goin' insane and now I feel it's a shame
And now I know it's insane, real love it ain't a game
It's power within the pain, and I don't know what to say
For hours I feel the ache, for hours throughout the day.

Sometimes I wanna go, sometimes I wanna stay
Sometimes I wanna get up, at times run away
But I'll never ever leave, you're mine, forever stay
So I'll just let it breathe and call it another day.

—Hours, Son of Kick

1

The stars weren't beautiful enough that night. And I wondered how that was possible? How could the stars seem ordinary? Spend three years on the terrace watching stars, as the nights pass along, and you might feel the same. When you're living a mundane life, a night spent lying under the open sky brings miraculous epiphanies. And you keep getting goose-bumps. Overwhelming happiness. But what if beauty becomes the norm? What remains beautiful then? Oh, if you don't love stars and the idea of gazing at them, well, stop existing, please.

As I was toying with this mind-boggling idea, feeling vain about my intellectual capabilities, my phone rang.

Pal pal dil ke paas tum…

And I picked up his call.

"Trick question – what will you find beautiful, if beauty is the norm?" I asked.

"When everything is beautiful, nothing is," he said.

"Said who?"

"Said Stanley Kubrick."

"That's why I love you. There's nothing you…"

"Listen, I think we should break up."

"… don't know. Damn, aren't you wondering why did I ask you so?"

"I think we should break up."

"Yeah, I know, the night gets you think… wait, what?"

"We should break up."

"What?"

"You are immature and too eccentric at times."

"What?"

"And you make love as if the apocalypse is about to strike."

"What?"

"Actually, no, what *really* bothered me yesterday was that you are fat as… fat as…"

"Fuck. No! Don't do this. I'll hit the gym this morning and start eating that salad you always wanted me to have. Don't do this! Fuck. I'll jog to your hostel, starting this morning. It was my first time. How was I supposed to know? I… I… um, I'm sorry I'm fat?"

"After pondering for a day, I have realized what I want."

"What?"

"A graceful lean lady who behaves in bed. Yesterday, it felt like a sumo was making love to a stick."

"Never miss a chance to wax eloquent. Oh, it's just a phase, it will pass. I'll start yoga, been delaying it since forever. You are *my* stick. And I love you sho much."

"No, you don't get it. It ends right here. You aren't attractive to me anymore."

"I…"

"No."

"Please…"

"No."

"Babe…"

"Goddammit, no."

"Is there anything I can say to keep you?"

"I'm afraid not."

"Okay. I'll find imperfection beautiful, when beauty is the norm."

"Huh?"

"Oh, fuck you!"

And I hung up.

Well, I *am* a panda. I mean, yeah one could have cloned him using my extra fat. And I guess I'd still be chubby, and not a graceful lean lady. And I wasn't going to jog or exercise or do yoga, I knew it. I wanted to make him stay somehow. I can't resist a bowl of ice-cream, man. I just can't. I love vanilla. Sigh!

But that's what he said was cute about me. He loved the tight squishy hugs I gave him. He didn't complain then. Did he use me for his bodily needs? Did he? That fucker!

Uh, no, I guess. It was I who wanted to make out. And I had set it up. Well, don't blame me. Blame James Cameron. He made that movie wherein a skinny, charming boy makes steaming hot love to the curvy woman (okay, not a panda of course, but a healthy analogy nonetheless), while the ship was sailing towards the iceberg. That's what planted the idea in my head.

I'm a strong independent woman who's proud of her appearance and is comfortable in her own skin. I believe in inner peace. And sound sleep. Because a good night's sleep brings radiance to your face, I've read. I'll get over this stupid breakup, I had thought. How bad could it be? I looked up at the stars, when I realized it's the past you are looking at when you are watching a star. And I didn't want to delve into the past. So I transferred my gaze from the stars of the past to the street-light of the present. I kept staring at it and gave way to my tears.

◆

I despised my roomies. Such arrogance, much hated. I was trying to get all emotional and sad by watching that movie where the husband dies, but leaves a bunch of letters for his wife to control her life even when he's dead. Yeah, so anyway, I had planned to choke myself, make a run for the terrace and cry in peace.

But my roomie girls, the girly girls, they ruined my carefully designed strategy by blabbering non-stop. Maybe I need a better set of noise-cancelling earphones. Either they keep talking of the latest nail-polish shade or the hottest guy to make out with. Oh, look at you guys, all wide-eyed and flattered. I got you, right? Haha, they don't discuss the latter one often. It's either nail polish or the hottest sale going on in town. I mean, they practically spend as much time as the shopkeepers themselves on FC road. And add to it the fact that all of them have near-hourglass figures. No, I shit you not. I hate all of them, so bloody fashionable and… and… pretty like that damn stick-guy wanted. Panda hates you. Such beauty, much hated.

I so wanted to have an ice-cream then. A bowl full of it. All I could think of was the way the chocolate melts in my mouth with every lick. It was driving me mad. I had to get an ice-cream. So, I got dressed and ran down to get one. While running, I came across a giant truck, and there were these laborers unloading some mirrors. I stopped there, looked at myself in the mirror. I noticed how the fat hung from my arms. I had no thigh gap and my face had two chins. I stepped back and ran back up.

Ultimately, I did end up on the terrace. All emotional and sad, crying in peace to get over my ex-boyfriend. No love, no chocolate ice-cream, no hourglass figure, no late-night calls, and no noise-cancelling earphones. Dear god, where was my life headed?

◆

I fiddled with my phone – to text or not to text, was the great question. The mornings, afternoons, and evenings are so easy to endure. But what about these nights?

Din dhal jaaye haaye, raat na jaaye,

Tu to na aye, teri yaad sataaye…

Retro songs never get old. What is the magic potion, I often wonder. Perhaps it was all soul, all music and no technology. Now it's all technology, part music and hardly any soul. That fat girl, whose name rhymes with '*Kaun-aak-chhi*', almost a panda herself, well gigantically less cute but slightly more famous than me, also claims to have sung a song. Yeah right! That was auto-tune, bitch.

My phone stared at me.

Sad weak miserable Nafisa: *Text him, dudette. He'll understand your withdrawal symptoms.*

Strong independent adult Nafisa: *No, you won't. Let him suffer your absence.*

Sad weak miserable Nafisa: *But what if he's not suffering? Shouldn't you check?*

Strong independent adult Nafisa: *Um…good question. But you don't need any pampering. You're a self-sufficient woman.*

Sad weak miserable Nafisa: *Oh, but you're missing him. Just this once. Hear from him, just one more time.*

Strong independent adult Nafisa: *Nope. This is the test of your self-control and resilience, lady.*

And then Screw It All Nafisa sent the text anyway. I had to find out. I put on my music and started the exercise routine of unlocking the phone five times a minute.

No reply arrived that night. I kept checking my phone again and again. But the patient girl that I was, I took only ten minutes to freak out. I cried myself to sleep that night. Goddammit, man, goddammit.

◆

The day of my admission was a day of revelation. Papa had noted down the address. The DD was prepared and we were good to go. Little did we know that we were leaving for a treasure hunt. PICT easily tops the list of the least easily 'findable' colleges of Pune. There was a high wall, a modest bus-stop followed by another tall wall to our left and a string of hotels, and breakfast joints to our right.

Papa stopped his bike and asked for PICT College. The commuters shrugged. We drove another ten feet to stop beside an auto-rickshaw driver.

"PICT?"

And again shoulders were shrugged. Looking at his face, one could have been easily fooled that there was no such college in existence. Not in the vicinity at least, no. So we went a full circle around Bharati Vidyapeeth only to arrive at the same spot again. Shoulders shrugged, yes. I got off the bike and happened to look at a helicopter whizzing through. With my eyes still on the sky, I started rotating when my eyes saw the giant PICT branding on top of a building. How could I miss that? I *grrred* at the commuters and the *auto wale kaka*. They were standing right outside my to-be-college and had no idea what lay behind the high wall.

There was a slope right where the wall ended, leading to the college gate. I stood at the gate and looked around. And a single 180-degree gaze was sufficient to cover the entire college campus. Damn, I had heard it was a small college, but that was tiny, like the Ant-Man of the colleges.

My mind was immediately bombarded with 'Your mama' kind of meme lines.

Your college so small that a single water tanker can flood the campus.

Your college so small that it admits only midgets.

Your college so small that a suicide by jumping off the building is out of syllabus.

Your college so small that it never enters a relationship because of space issues.

I had fought with my parents to let me stay in the hostel for my engineering tenure. I wanted to move out of the comfort of my home and live life on my own terms. I had promised mumma a visit every week. Papa argued that it was a bad investment and it was insane to have a home in Pune and yet opt for a hostel. I countered his argument by mentioning that I was their only child and they were free to reduce the budget of my wedding by that amount. That shut him up.

Well, I hate to admit this, but the first feeling I ever had for my college was humiliation. So I had just chanted *Ganpati Bappa Moraya* and gone ahead for the admission with papa, hoping that the future four years would wipe away that humiliation and replace it with ill-placed pride.

◆

It was one of those days when you walk around like a zombie and have no memory of the day that went by. Yes, I did smile, wave at people, stare at average looking guys, yawn during boring lectures, cringe at the messy mess' lunch, played the dumb dumb-charades after college, cringe again at the messy mess' dinner, oh wait, I do remember the day, then. Oops.

So there I was, sitting on Bharati Vidyapeeth's footpath after the customary solitary walk. I so relished that walk. Such wow, much like. It's a straight stretch of road flanked by concrete buildings, gulmohar trees, flowers, and birds. An enchanting experience, no matter how your mood is. A visual metaphor for our mundane lives. Brilliant green followed by dull gray followed by gorgeous orange followed by duller gray.

Tears simply arrived on their own that night. I hadn't even noticed myself sobbing. I wanted to run back and hide under my blanket, safe from the world, but I could not. Cupping my face, I realized the problem was with me. I was unhappy inside. And I didn't know how to undo that. I felt something nudging. It was a white dog. I hated dogs. I simply could not stand them. One had bitten mumma for no apparent fault of hers and thus the hatred was born. Greedy bastards! They do nothing, lying there in mud all day with creepy insects. She nudged at my arm again and I tried to shoo her away.

But she sat at my feet and her eyes sparkled when they met mine. I was hypnotized. How was I better than her? I sat, cried and did nothing to change whatever made me unhappy. I looked at her again and her eyes were smiling at me. I got off the footpath and hugged her like an old friend. I know she liked it too.

Dogs just don't lie gathering dust, chasing cars, barking incessantly; sometimes when humans fail, these furry beings come to our rescue.

2

Time on your side that will never end
The most beautiful thing you can ever spend
But you work in a shirt with your name tag on it
Drifting apart like a plate tectonic
It don't matter to me
'Cause all I wanted to be
Was a million miles from here
Somewhere more familiar...

I gulped down another bottle of beer as Lily Allen's 'Oh My God' played on a loop in my ears. Okay, it was Mark Ronson's song featuring Lily but that lady owned that song, so yeah, the other way round for me. Having loved that one, I had explored the rest of Lily's songs and surprisingly none of them were as charismatic. Her voice was still cheeky and fun, but nothing like this one. Maybe that's how the crescendo of your life builds up. Nobody else could have sung it like Lily, but it took her a host of above-average songs to make that one happen and make me go wow. So keep singing, keep doing the shit you do because the wow moment is out there, waiting to happen. God, Lily was sexy as hell. She had become my lady crush.

I was quite high by then; the one I had thrown off the terrace was the sixth beer bottle. The walls walked me back to my room.

"Where's Pia? It's midnight already," I asked, standing by the door.

"She has gone on a date, maybe it is going too well," Aditi answered, with a wink.

"What? A date? But she was single till this afternoon, right?"

"Yeah, she still is."

"Then?"

"Our babe set up a date via that sick new dating app."

"Which app?"

"It rhymes with hinder."

"What? That long a name for an app?"

And as if *she* was drunk, skipping my question, she simply continued, "Oh, it's damn cool, man. People pop up with their photos and a bio. You swipe right if you like someone and left if you wanna pass. That's it. If the guy has already swiped you right, which he most probably has already, then it's a match and you guys can start chatting. Simple as that. Oh yeah, if you really liked someone and can't wait to talk to him, you can send a superlike, once every twelve hours though. Neat, right?"

I was burning inside with envy, and partly because of the alcohol. While that bitch was perhaps making out with her date, I was walking on earth, drinking beer and feeling miserable, utterly unaware of that mind-boggling invention. I had resolved to install the brilliant app with the weird long name 'It rhymes with hinder' and start the manhunt ASAFP.

Feeling triumphant, I had started to walk for my bed when I suddenly felt a tangy liquid in my mouth. And I threw up on Pia's bed, having turned my panda body just in time to save my own bed. Well, that was mostly because of the envy and partly because of the alcohol.

◆

My bed looked like a crime scene – sheets and my pajamas covered with blood. I got up and wiped off the drool from my face. The room smelled fine though. Wonder what Aditi did after I had puked and crashed. Alcohol is wondrous in such matters – builds great immunity for the lamest joke, foulest smell, worst advice, etc.

Come to think of it, alcohol turns you into the universe. You don't give a fuck as well once high.

I moaned in pain, pressing my belly. The cramps had kicked in. And it was already 10:30 a.m. Better stay in bed, skip college and pray for some mercy, I decided.

A sanitary napkin placed and I was ready for all the stuff they don't show you in those lame-ass TV commercials. Man, that girl wants to play tennis, report tsunamis, look beautiful, jump and run – basically conquer the world on the day she's on her period. And all that by just placing a sanitary napkin on her vagina or pussy or whatever.

I hooked my phone with a charger and opened the app store. Searched for 'It rhymes with hinder' and found nothing. Searched for it. Nothing. Rhymes with hinder. Nothing. Tried with 'inder' then and I struck gold. That bitch could have just told me the correct name. No brownie points for dealing with my vomit the previous night. Girl remained a bitch for me.

I connected the account with the most time-killing and mind-killing cyber invention of the century. Yeah yeah, that website with 'book' in it and not being even remotely connected with a book. Boom. Profiles started popping up and I was good to go. So, I went on a swiping spree. To the right, they went. And within a few minutes, every right swipe made the screen say 'It's a match'. And I was bombarded with radiantly average messages like 'hi', 'hello' to downright creepy 'hey babe', 'phone number give *na*', 'how about we meet and do naughty things?', etc.

Unmatch. Unmatch. Unmatch. Wow, it was an army of retards waiting to pounce. Then I realized that people had a space assigned for their bio as well. Damn, no guy till then had had a bio and my first criterion was set. No right swipe without a quirky bio. Turns out they had time to click selfies with buffaloes, exotic cars, photoshopped actresses, but a few finger taps on the god-forbidden keyboard – too much to expect.

So, I went on a swiping spree again. To the left, they went. Goddammit, someone write a bio already, man. And soon it said 'There's no one new around you'. Grrr. I was about to explode. Such frustration, much pain, no wow.

I curled my body into a ball and was brought to tears by the cramps. Yet I could not figure out what to pray for – periods to vanish or a bio to appear. Man, I needed sleep, a boyfriend, and a painkiller badly. Times like these and I feel being a woman sucks. Sucks sucks sucks.

◆

I was walking back to the hostel after the last class of the day. Was really sleepy, yawned a large yawn and opened the app that rhymed with hinder. And on it, popped up the yummiest guy I had laid my eyes on. Man, he made me stop walking. My eyes were wide again and sleep… what sleep?

Okay, the guy was ticking every checkbox along the way.

Bio? Yes. Here you go:

Amar is in Engineering college and has no idea what to do with his life. So he spends his time in the gym, clubs and dance floors. As you might observe, he has high regards for personal hygiene and his body. His beard shall always be perfectly trimmed. Don't judge him yet though, he's not another dumb guy with muscles, rather a gentleman. Free bike rides for the girl who swipes him right. Single, single all the way.

He didn't seem dumb. I tried judging him, but he had described himself in third person in the bio. That's the last stunt I would expect a gym junkie to pull off.

Hot? Yes, very.

Cat eyes and long eyebrows that extended into eternity. You would notice those immediately after you've drooled over his chiseled biceps. I swiped to the next picture and there he was, teasing us love-famished girls with a sneak peek of those abs. His face was almond shaped with no cheek fat whatsoever and hence an accentuated jawline. Black hair and a classy hairdo to go with it. No fuss there. He was tall, well so was I, but he looked taller than me. Beard perfectly trimmed, just like he had promised.

Come to think of it, a well-maintained beard and a sexy selfie are achievements guys and girls aspire towards these days. Narcissistic much? Well, a debate for another day perhaps. I don't care as long as my guy looks kissable. Frankly, that guy looked well out of my league.

Okay, I know – this too good to be true guy, how could he possibly be single? I wanted to solve the mystery.

I *had* to do it, there was no other way – superliked the guy. I just *had* to pounce and call dibs on him first, as I secretly kept praying for a city-wide app crash on ladies' phones.

The phone was still in my palm and as I reached the hostel gate, it beeped. The bystanders wondered why I had jumped with joy. Well, how could I not? It was a match!

3

Amar: *I was told that a guy never gets a superlike. Ever.*

Nafisa: *Man, I'm a feminist. And a man can't have monopoly on superlikes.*

He: *Thank you. I'm assuming you're single, then.*

Me: *No shit, Sherlock. First things first, how come you are single?*

He: *I broke up a year ago. Working on myself since then.*

Me: *As in?*

He: *As in these abs didn't exist a year ago.*

Me: *Sounds like a sob story. Let's reserve that for later. No, I meant how come no girl got hold of you here?*

He: *I just created the account. You got lucky, it seems. But I appreciate the intent shown. Was quite bold.*

Me: *Okay phew, umm, I don't wanna sound desperate or anything, but you're totally hot. And I so wanna date you right now, I'd fly down at your place if I were Shaktimaan.*

He: **cough* *cough* Only date me? :p*

Me: *Yeah, for now. I'm a sanskaari Indian lady. What else did you expect?*

He: **cough* sanskaari *cough**

Me: *Oh, who am I kidding, I would totally shag you, dude.*

He: *That bad, is it?*

Me: *The sanskaari version keeps reminding me that it's fine, but the horny me is kinda raging these days and I shouldn't be confessing this on our first chat, but to hell with that, it's the truth.*

He: *Whatever is natural is perverted and vice versa. Being horny is not a sin, nobody's judging you. At least I don't. I was as miserable as you, a year ago.*

Me: *Man oh man, killing two stones with one bird, eh? Those abs can talk. I sound miserable right now?*

He: *Desperate and miserable, yes. But I guess that's K? We all are, after a breakup.*

Me: *K? K what? The letter before L, the letter after J? JK stands for Just Kidding, so did you mean 'Kidding'? Or K as in potassium? K as in I can KO you? Knock you out and feed to the sharks perhaps? Shark has K in it.*

He: *Chill, will you?*

Me: *Okay. I'm not a grammar nazi, but can you swipe over your keyboard a bit more to include an 'okay' instead of K. That single letter gets on my nerves.*

He: *Okay. Happy? You are already suggesting changes, not a good sign.*

Me: *Hahaha. You want me to tease you like them strong independent women?*

He: *I would hate that. I like the miserable you. So, when are we making out?*

Me: *And I was the horny one, eh? What did your breakup teach you? My answer depends on yours now.*

He: *I've learnt to love me, enjoy my own company, be comfortable on long bike rides alone and invest time in being a well-groomed gentleman. The product of all those lessons is the profile that fetched me a superlike. Guess I did fine then.*

Me: *Come pick me up right now. And I mean now. K?*

He: *K :)*

No points for guessing we made out later that night. A 'wall-banging, stationery-smashing, screaming mad, can't-get-hands-off-you' make out session. God, he knew his game well. Smelled like a man, kissed like a passionate dream and groped like a wild caring gentleman. His well-trimmed beard was a pain in my ass figuratively, face literally. Anyway, screw all that, it was relief at last for me. *Achhe din aa gaye the.* We had gone to a club, gotten drunk and driven to his place before all of that, of course.

◆

We were both panting frantically, lying half-naked on his bed, rather a double-bed created by joining together his and roomie's bed. I reached for his hand and placed his palm gently on my bosom that shielded my heart from popping out. His sort of rugged skin's touch on my sensitive nipple made me moan a bit. Skin on skin felt sensational, to be honest. I could relate with those who associate meditation with orgasm; didn't seem bullshit anymore. And I placed my palm on his heart which was sorta jogging, not even running.

"Player, haan?"

"No, I'm just..." he shook his head, shrugging his shoulders, said, "...can you pass me a smoke?"

He lit one up and looked out of the window. I didn't know what to do, so I got up and searched for my t-shirt and realized that he had torn it in the process earlier. I grabbed a loose shirt of his and looked at him again while buttoning it up. His cat eyes were glistening and a tear came rolling down his cheek as he exhaled the smoke. He was still shirtless, oblivious of my admiring stare at his sculpted muscles and abdomen. Freedom of a bra-less existence, I tell you. I had calmed down enough for a second shag session, but that just seemed selfish.

So I snuck up beside him, cupped his wet cheek and gave a peck on the dry one, ensuring to prolong the peck a little.

And he opened up, "When the rush settled down, it hit me that it was *you* lying in my bed, not her. My ex, I mean. I didn't want all of this. The version of Amar you see right now is a result of hatred and revenge. She dumped me because I wasn't classy enough for her. My dressing sense wasn't up to the mark, my English wasn't refined, I lacked confidence and she just felt embarrassed being with me. The fact that I loved her wasn't enough apparently. And thus the transformation happened. I was on a diet of protein shakes, quality movies, stylish TV series and long rides with my beloved bike."

"Books?"

He chuckled and said, "Not my thing, sorry. Don't have the patience to read those; I'd happily consume a movie instead."

"Never mind, I'm guessing we won't be talking much anyway when together."

He planted a peck on my cheek then.

"Why the tears then? I mean, you hate her, right? That's what drove you, isn't it?"

"One wishes for it, but love never evaporates like that. Rather it should not, if you claim it was the real deal. Yes, I *do* hate her because she left me. And yet, I think, she has never left me."

I gestured for him to pass the smoke and took a long drag.

Exhaling smoke rings, I said, "Don't be a prisoner of your mind and petty emotions. No doubt, the version of Amar I made out with is better than the one she dumped a year ago. But unless you get over her, the idea of your hatred driving you, those tears shall keep recurring. Perhaps, it was the passion to see a better version of you that fired you up. Often, hatred for people is confused with love for self. I believe, it was the latter pushing you. If that's not the case, then you lied to me last evening about having learnt from your breakup, because you're still as miserable then, under all those distractions of a desirable body and trimmed beard. Fuck that bitch and fuck your idea of true love. I'll evaporate that stupid obsession and cook yummy momos with that steam. Move on, okay?"

"I will. You'll stay, right?" he had asked that with those shiny wet greenish eyes. Man, he looked so cute and vulnerable at that moment.

I took a hasty drag and gave him a puffy smoky kiss. We groped and kissed for a while more, while sharing the cancerous smoke, before we dozed off for the night.

◆

I texted Amar: *Panda hungry. Panda need something yummy.*

He didn't text back immediately. So I called him and got third time lucky.

"Check the text and reply."

"Huh?"

And I hung up. It was 7 a.m.

He texted: *You're one annoying babe. On my way.*

I chuckled and replied: *Autocorrect here. Bitch, you meant bitch.*

He looked sexier with unkempt hair and his beard a tad all over the place. It was as if his secret was revealed. I walked up to kiss him good morning, but he yawned and exhaled unkissable breath.

"Dude, your mouth stinks."

"Fuck you. Panda was hungry, wasn't it? I was afraid of falling asleep driving here."

"A mouthwash wouldn't have hurt. Or carry gums hereafter."

"Shut up, dude. I'm still sleepy as a… uhm… that cute animal… uh…"

"Koala, honey."

I pulled both his cheeks, gave a peck on both and became the pillion rider.

"Where we headed to?"

"To the best *sambar-wada* of Pune that I have tasted. You'll find one of your kinds there."

The chilly wind gave me a couple of goosebumps, so I snuggled up to him a bit more.

My tummy was growling and to cover up the embarrassingly loud sound, I asked, "Do you feel important?"

"Uh, I'm still sleepy and the club can't handle that right now."

"Okay well, last night I was sitting on Bharati Vidyapeeth's footpath after my customary walk. And so many people pass you by. It's almost overwhelming. But then I noticed that almost everyone had company for the walk – wife, friend, babe and pets. And I realized, nobody wants to die unimportant. We fear it like the worst fate that could be cursed upon us. We want to matter to someone. The feeling of nobody being beside your grave, that 'who will cry when you die' shit creates this craving to be loved. We need the assurance that people would care if you were to disappear tomorrow."

"Nafisa, is this really important? I mean, right now?"

"Yes, babe. Right now, yes. I need to puke it all out. Yeah so, the million dollar question is, what about us? The average folks? Those who don't have any passion in life, aren't extraordinary in anything – not even existing. No dreams to pursue, happy with the daily *chakkipeesing* and *peesing* and *peesing* of life. What about us? We don't excel in studies, nor do we fail. We are right there in the middle of the struggle, wondering whether to be disillusioned by the dreamers or embrace the hopelessness of losers. We aren't so good and we ain't too bad either. We're average. How do we become important for someone? We won't be creating vaccines, helping eradicate poverty or reducing global warming."

"Agreed. Enlighten me, keep going."

"All that philosophy tells us is that we have a purpose in here. But what about those who'll never figure out why or what? We are the consumers of all those memorable novels, badass quotes, heartbreaking movies and the psychologically potent ads targeted at us. We are never going to create. We'll die consuming. We'd be part of that million odd herd that fills up the stadiums for concerts. We'll never be among those hand-picked artistic folks on the damn stage, playing that goddamned groovy music. How do we die peacefully, knowing that our life mattered for someone?"

We reached our destination, the entrance of Inox, Bund Garden, and man, was that place brimming with hoomans or what! The two guys operating the roadside shop looked like brothers to me. One was busy frying the *wadas* while another served. Amar went ahead to order a couple of plates of *sambar-wada* and pointed his eyebrows towards them mouthing 'Watch it'.

So a fresh batch of wada dough went into the piping hot oil and then began the *jugalbandi*.

"Oh baby baby, tinge podilasadama…"

"Da!"

"Oh lady lady, sunitangarimatama…"

"Da!"

Okay, I didn't get the words past baby baby and lady lady, so just filling them up with my hypothetical shit, but what I enjoyed was how the serving 'assumed' brother completed his wada frying brother's beat with 'Da' and their rhythm forced a smile outta me. Batch finished, song finished and wadas were ready to be sacrificed to the hungry panda's growling tummy. And ooh la la, were they delicious or what! The best sambar with the softest wadas ever.

"They're indeed good, Amar."

"Autocorrect here. Best, you mean best."

I ate up nearly the entire batch. I was *that* hungry and they were *that* yummy. We didn't talk on our way back as I laid my head on his shoulder, my eyes closed, snuggled up to him.

And then he said, "Our existence only makes sense if we force it to. So, although we know we are the average ones who'll die an average death, having retired from our average jobs and having lived an average life with an average wife bringing up average kids, it's better to die believing that we made the people around us happy. That someone smiled because of me, lived another day because of me, loved because of me."

"What about those who never marry or stay alone all along?"

"I can only wish that they make themselves happy. Yes, we aren't important to the universe. But we only need to love one person truly to make peace with that harsh truth. It can be your average lover or the average wife or the average you yourself, but love them and become a part of their story of existence. So whenever you die, you'll take away a piece of their heart that could never be replaced or repaired. It would remain damaged and love-torn. Because, though we are all average, each one is a unique average."

I made him stop the bike by hastily tapping his shoulders, got down and kissed his stinking sambar-ish mouth for what seemed like an eternity.

4

We were supposed to go for a beach outing in the morning. Goa heats up pretty soon during noon. But the lazy fucks that we were – both of us remained in bed and asked the room-boy to bring us a carton of chilled beer.

He leaned in to kiss me, but we still smelled of dirt, the dirty mattress and sweat. I wonder how those movie stars make the lying-down-in-bed-horizontal-face-kisses look so lovely. Let me tell you, it's one awkward position to kiss someone. I felt like a fish gasping for breath. So I pushed him away and pointed to the bathroom.

"Well, how about we take a bath together?" he asked.

"Hmm," I mused and kissed him anyway.

The room-boy kept banging the door while we were busy doing everything other than bathing in the bathroom.

We were clothed again, smelling of saliva, semen and soap. Chilled beer, boyfriend by my side, a portable speaker, laptop and then began the magic of Coldplay. Heaven on my tongue, heaven in my ears, what a day, oh!

Call it magic
Call it true
Call it magic

When I'm with you
And I just got broken,
Broken into two
Still I call it magic,
When I'm next to you

Amar got up and sang along, stripping for me. I waved my index finger a no no and told him to just dance. Coldplay music reminds me of the stars. I immediately imagined myself in their live concert, swaying to their tunes under a starry sky.

And I don't, And I don't, And I don't, And I don't,
No, I don't it's true,
I don't, no I don't, no I don't, no I don't,
Want anybody else but you

God, he came down on his knees and asked me for a dance.

"Are you drunk already or really romantic?"

"Shut up, let's dance. Coldplay wants us to."

I put my arms around his neck and he put his around my waist. Okay, he tried to. It was quite a waist, you know. He pulled me closer and was able to interlock his fingers finally.

Few bottles, songs, kisses, toe-crushing moves later, I was tipsy. I felt like a feather. My balance fluid had gone for a little spin, but I wasn't hammered yet. *Balance fluid*, yeah! Science, bitches!

This tipsy feeling is the perfect phase of being drunk. I remember who I am kissing and yet my feet are in the clouds. One more sip and the tipsy turns into a headache. And frankly, I was taking in a lot more than a sip. So the perfect phase didn't last long and I was soon puking.

I washed up and came back to dance a bit more, but my baby was already busy snoring.

And as I stood at the bathroom door with the dizziness vanishing with each passing moment, I pondered – was it just a fling for them lusty hormones or something chemically serious, as Coldplay's 'Yellow' played on the speaker:

Your skin, oh yeah your skin and bones,
Turn into something beautiful,
Do you know,
You know I love you so,
You know I love you so.

Anyway, high of an alcohol lives fast, dies young. But the big daddy was to arrive later that night. Shit was gonna get real.

◆

"Amaaaaaaaaaaaaaar, I can't lift my face, yaar. It's glued to the pillow."

And that bastard started laughing and laughed for an eternity.

"Come help me, yaar. It's not funny."

"I'm trying to come to you. But my stomach is glued to the floor."

So even I started laughing, and we laughed for like forever.

Rewind to a couple hours before that.

I was having my waist tattooed, a little above the bum. The tattoo? *Amar prem.*

Go ahead, judge me for being cheesy. But hey, I had it all planned, you know. If things went haywire with Amar, I could always claim that the tattoo was a result of *Andaz Apna Apna* fandom. Yeah, beat that!

The tattoo guy asked us if we'd like to buy *gaanja*. Who the fuck says no to that?

Rewind to an hour after that.

Amar was preparing joints for us, separating the seeds from the weed. The portable speaker was playing mothafucking Snoopy DO double-G and the sickest gangsta rap beats by Dr Dre. My guy knew how to set the mood for things. Had a playlist for every occasion. By the way, he played dubstep when we made out. Bangarang, to be specific, the bad, bad pun intended of course.

I took a long drag from the first one.

"Hmm, nothing. Where is the kick?" I asked.

"It will work. There will be a tip-off point. Enjoy the music and keep pulling."

"Okay, fuck that. Who would win if Hulk and Ant-Man fight?"

"Wow, where did this come from?"

"Answer *na*. Think think."

"Hulk can't be killed, I guess. But he needs to locate Ant-Man first. I wonder if Ant-Man's punches would even move that green beast."

"Okay, here's my theory. Ant-Man would win. He can just enter Hulk's nose or ear and irritate him to death. Hulk would keep getting angry and perhaps smash himself to pieces. Gigantic and powerful isn't always the solution."

"What is love?"

"Wow! Now where did *that* come from, babe?"

"You know, just. Are we simply screwing around? I know it must have crossed your mind as well. Are we a thing?"

"Well, we're having a great time together. And I don't wanna define our thing. Love? Fling? Friends with benefits? Who cares? But let me tell you something. You have nothing to be insecure about. Your looks alone can kill and would have them shallow girls swooning over you. And you have a sweet, sweet heart beating right here. You'll have to do something drastically fucked up to push me away. Why did you ask that?"

"I think about us and all I can remember is making out, kisses, beers and dance. I felt, is that significant enough for you? Where's the philosophical connection between us? The wavelength that needs to match, as they say."

"Oh god, you're adorable, come here," I said and pulled him in for a smoky kiss.

I put my arm over his shoulder and said, "Don't you remember my dimples when you make me laugh, the assuring hug on that hill during that pretty sunrise, the love in my eyes when you brought me chocolate brownie at three in the morning. I'll tell you what's love. Love is the dark circles you see here, under my eyes. Love is when I don't mind dark circles for a night of your voice in my ears. The definition of love for us keeps changing. Love tomorrow might be a responsible adult or a philosophy spewing artist or a bad boy who breaks hearts, but it is beers and kisses and dance for me right now. And you just fit the bill, babe."

We kept staring at each other, sort of competing who would blink first. And then my neck started tilting back. I could not control it. I clenched my teeth, squeezed my eyes and tried to push it ahead, but the neck just kept tilting back.

Oh god, someone had turned time into a 0.5x Youtube video. I could feel my eyeballs scanning left to right, sloooooowly, while my neck continued doing a see-saw back and forth. I took ages to turn my neck and check for Amar. I didn't realize when he had slipped out of my arms. I screamed for his name and he said, "I'm swimming, down here."

He was swimming on the dry floor, waving his arms and legs, asking me to join him. I was on my knees in a doggy position, watching him. I was afraid of putting my leg down – the floor seemed so far away. So I decided to lie down. But I couldn't change my position, so I just kept rotating on my knees and palms, figuring out how to go about it.

"Amar, I can't sleep. I'm a dog right now, but wanna sleep like that inverted cockroach."

"Roooooooollll over *na*."

So I rolled like a dog and was finally on my back with my arms and legs still in the air. It was a slo-mo movie, I swear. I could give birth to my grandchildren in the time it took me to bring my arms down.

My neck kept going round and round with the ceiling fan.

"Amar, I think I see Batman in that right top corner of our room."

"Really? Where? Where?"

"See, he's flapping his wings also."

"I think that's a fly. You are so stupid and fat," he said and laughed uncontrollably.

"Am I so stupid and fat? Boo hoo hoo," I was reduced to tears immediately and even I blurted out the truth to him, "you look terrible as well. I hate your abs and cat eyes and sweet nature. I hate them. Hate 'em hate 'em hate 'em, but you're so hot and hot and vulnerable. Come here, make love to me."

I raised my arms, waiting for him to arrive in them.

Fast forward to the beginning of the chapter.

My head glued to the pillow and his stomach glued to the floor. We did try to go out for dinner later that night, walking side by side, hands held firmly. But we saw the traffic and they were like missiles with head-lights. We looked at each other, dropped our necks and stumbled back to the room. Both of us crashed on the bed while Dr Dre kept playing on the speakers.

Weed had kicked in and how! Not to mention that it almost ruined our trip. Even a door knock felt like a bazooka strike on the wood. The spinning room syndrome remained for another day and all we could do was blabber and laugh in our hotel room. That's the Goa I witnessed on my trip – coconut trees from the bus window, hotel room, ceiling fan, room-boy, a tattoo shop and a fly that resembled Batman.

Quora, huh? Amar had told me about this website after one of our love-making sessions. So I had created an account and was surfing my way around. Questions that need answers. How stupid that is!

Okay, so I was in a mood to kill and raring to hunt down quirky questions.

My eyes lit up when I saw 'Is tinder good for girls?'

I rubbed my palms and started screwing the keyboard.

Answer:

I am a girl (yay!) And I'm on tinder (Umm... wow. Awkward.)

So, most people think 'the app that rhymes with hinder' is better for girls for they get a lot more matches than them boys.

Pretty true, I don't deny it.

But here's the thing, you can only find a match when two parties swipe right and we girls, being picky as we are, choose either hot ones or smart ones.

Perhaps even a superlike if both (Yeah, it's not a myth. My boyfriend can testify.)

Do you really think we wouldn't swipe right a decent looking smart guy?

Like, se-ri-ous-ly?!

Now, how would I know that you're a smarty pants and look kissable? A bio to go with your naked abs as well. Yes, there's space for both.

PS - Girls like me do analyze that bio before swiping. Work on it. Please.

Love! :)

I clicked on the 'submit' button and popped a window asking for the bio I'd like to accompany my answer with. Turned out, you could customize the bio line for every new answer. Well okay. I typed in: *37 swipes/minute.*

And there I had my first Quora answer. Way to go, dudette! I had smelled blood and kept hunting.

Next question: Is it normal to hate someone without any reason?

Answer:

Let me tell you something that happened last week.

A regular Sunday evening out with mumma. I wanted to buy a black shirt. Generic black shirt. No designs or fancy collars. We stopped at a shop. XL size. Regular length. Black shirt.

"You like it?" Mumma asked.

I nodded a loud and clear no.

What was not to like? Was a freaking shirt that was black, just the way I wanted it. But nah! Didn't like it. And no matter how hard I try, I can't really justify my choice.

There are some things you just like. They make you feel good. And you instantly want it. Like that sky blue shirt instead.

And there are some things you just don't like... like that black, ah, never mind.

Mumma was pretty mad at me for buying a red tee eventually.

Gist of all that is what you feel is pretty normal. You don't have to like people. Need not smile always just because people think it's beautiful. Hate them all you want, but then love gave us Rehmans, Gandhis and Mandelas, what did baseless hatred gift us? Right, world wars.

Hope that answers your question.

Love! :)

One more for the night and I was to call it a day.

Last question: How do you find your life's purpose?

Answer:

Ah! Another guy in the 12th. Another guy who is going to be forced into Engineering. Another soul shall wake up with regret.

Here's what you can do:

A. You're an Indian guy. Pursue Engineering. Get a job at TCS as a Software Engineer. Then run after an MBA. When you finally make some money, get married. Have kids, wait till they have kids again and die in peace.

B. You're an Indian guy. Break stereotypes. Be a rebel. Do what makes you happy. Choose Humanities or Diploma in Dance. Umm, be a painter or photographer. You might regret it, but then who doesn't. Lose that inhibition, follow your intuition, free your inner soul and break away from tradition.

"Practically kya karu?" You might be screaming at me by now.

Sit down with a paper. Write everything you love!

Pizza. Chocolate. That chick from your college. Reading. Dancing – everything!

Let's get it started (ha!), let's get it started in here. Yeah.

Dare to dream. Now is the time.

Love! :)

And I was done. The keyboard had had enough. I felt happy, to be honest. Writing helpful answers could have fetched me few good karma points. Lazy social service, I guess. I sent a voice note to Amar with a kiss in it and dozed off. Night night.

◆

My phone was buzzing with notifications next morning. Quite a people had taken liking to my answers and upvoted them. Not thousands, not even hundreds, only twenty or so, but I guess it was a start.

I wasn't going to college since it was *that time of the month*, so as the stereotype goes I was happy, angry, confused, mad, violent and a bitch, just like a woman should be. Amar was in the class, stuck on the first bench. That's all he texted me. So I opened my newly discovered obsession.

Question: What are some things you love doing in college that can't be done at home?

Answer:

Is it honesty hour? I guess, it is. I like texting. Let me take a step beyond and declare that ***I love my phone****.*

There! I said it! Go tell my mom, if you must.

Okay, so I declare this hour as honesty hour.

*How many of us have texted our boyfriends under the desk? *raises right hand**

*How many of us have bunked college 'cause we spent the previous night talking to our sweetheart? *raises left hand**

How many of us have a college group on 'the app that's a pun on What's up'? Aaaarrgghhh! You feel me now? It's on mute, isn't it?

How many of us have used the 'Sorry mumma, I had to attend an extra lecture', when we were actually at the cheapest nearest single screen theater?

Should I stop already?!

Bottom line is – we all have the same, stupid, boring college. And we love it. And we flaunt our college t-shirts no matter how old or shabby they might be.

To finish it off with a personalized quote – College doesn't teach us to pass exams, it teaches us to be prepared for one.

Cheers to your alma mater! Love! :)

Question: Is the condition of the boy's hostel showed in TVF Pitchers true?

Answer:

I moved to a girl's hostel three years back and still kinda hate it. Girls are a bit too girly to handle and honestly quite boring. So I spend most of my time on the terrace, watching stars and thinking about life.

I had already noticed the adjacent boys' hostel but never really cared about what happened in there until that night when I saw them boys playing cricket in the corridor. That wasn't the only thing I noticed. They were all shirtless, with only boxers thrown on. I giggled at first and watched them for a while. I even caught a couple of guys smoking on the terrace of their hostel.

A few days later, when I was on the terrace, talking to my boyfriend, I heard the sound of glass cracking. I leaned over to see. Them guys again, fooling around. Only this time, they were throwing empty beer bottles from second floor. The air was filled with the laughter and the constant whistling of the watchman there. Ever since, I've wanted to sneak into their hostel.

I managed to make friends, though, who download movies for me. Even guys who share some amazing porn. Hostelites who know where I can find food at 2 a.m. but none courageous enough to help me sneak in.

And to answer your question, we will never know what the real thing is 'cause what happens in the hostel, more often than not, stays in the hostel.

Love! :)

And then I found the gem of them all, a question so Indian and quirky, it would win hands down in a pageant for questions.

Question: How do we say '*Ye paani maine upar se piya hai*' in English?

Answer:

*Wow! Does this thing still exist! I mean, AIDS paani ki bottle share karne se to nahi failta yaar. *Just kidding, don't kill me**

Anyway, to answer your question, next time someone asks you, you can say, "I haven't soiled the bottle." It means that you haven't contaminated it with your saliva.

Absolutely loved the question though. Love! :)

That's when I sneezed and it was blood all over again. I curled up in a ball to cry and curse womanhood.

◆

I was reading on the not-so-stupid-now website with them questions and answers. Wait, its name started with Q and ended with A. Hmm, interesting. Well played, Quora, well played. I kept scrolling as the epiphany faded away.

Question: What happened to the art of letters?

Answer:

We became serial scrollers. That's what we became. We killed innocent letters somewhere. Look at the miserable us now. Everyone stares at a screen, neck hanging low as if in submission. You own cellphones? No. Cellphones own you.

Swiping fingers on a screen. Where's the art in that? Where's the enchanting paper smell? Where are those little curves of your cursive handwriting? Etched on paper, etched on my heart. We're all guilty, we've killed the innocent letters.

Nobody knows of patience. The eagerness associated with a postman's arrival on his modest bicycle. Wonder what that is, right? What postman? And a bicycle, meh! Handwriting is an extension of your personality, they say. Where's that extension now? Yeah, rotting somewhere beneath those 'tap tap tap' fingers. Fuck those goddamned emojis and stickers. Fuck them till the end of the world.

How did the charm of pen and paper perish? Give it up for the criminal – technology. It brought people closer, the voice of a distant relative on that receiver and hell broke loose. The anti-evolution of our attention span began. And now, memories are first stored on the phone, rather than being registered with naked eyes. You see those jam-packed stadiums with people holding up glowing mobile screens? Yeah, it's not beautiful, it's terrifying and sad.

Some people are still holding on to the letters, I hope. Old school boys and old school girls. And the old school romance of letters. Writing that gives me goosebumps right now. Quorans are a different species, but what about the rest of the nation, rest of the world? More pen-pals, please. Mother Earth can do without a few trees. Let's put the paper to good use. Send a letter to someone right now. Now, you bloody murderers.

Okay, that was quite a rant. And I loved the guy's name, to be honest. Kiaan. I hovered the cursor over his name and popped a mini window displaying his bio.

Kiaan- Splashing the world with the colors of brilliance. Painter, who often ends up writing. And an old school guy, out and out.

I messaged him.

Me: I'm guilty as well. Here to confess a crime and ask for forgiveness. I love texting. Yeah, you heard that right. But, having said that, I crave the charm of ink on paper. Be my pen-pal?

He: Okay, I hate you already. Better write me a madly brilliant letter and I shall write you back.

Love your name though. Nafisa.

Me: Me loves your name more. Kiaan. Your language and the over-emphasis on 'Fuck' seems familiar though.

He: Madam, there's not much to differentiate between grammar lovers/nazis in the virtual space. Everyone writes perfect English. So my personal extension – cuss words.

Me: Same pinch, painter. Wait for that letter, then. Ciao.

So we ended up exchanging our college addresses. I kept wondering what to write to him. Mad yet brilliant, huh? Amar texted me later that night, he had booked tickets for NH7 Weekender. Screw the letter, I thought and called up my boyfriend and made a college record of uttering 'I love you' seventy-seven times on the phone.

6

"What are you afraid of?"

"Well, I've never done it before."

"It will be okay. There's always a first time. Don't worry. This won't hurt much. Trust me."

"If you say so. But I'm quite hesitant about it."

"Once I set my eyes on something, I work hard and get it. It hurts at first, but get past it and the experience will be great."

No, that wasn't a motivational self-help speech going on. Amar and I were watching the famous porn series wherein a girl enters as a *sanskaari* virgin and exits as an *apavitra naari*. And the guy in action, oh my, what an actor! I had never seen a porn plot loaded with meaningful dialogues. Those opening ones can make it easily to any feel-good inspiring movie.

Usually, porn logic is pretty straightforward:

Car broke down in the middle of a deserted road? Let's have sex.

Pizza guy knocks and you walk up to the door with no cash? Let's have sex.

Son's hunk of a friend visits you to talk about homework? Let's have sex.

Your step-daughter doesn't wake up by herself? Let's have sex.

Okay, so we needed porn guidance for it was decision time for us. Should we lose that priced virginity? We weren't even drunk. So our conscience wasn't exactly numbed down. It wasn't the first time we were in bed together, but that was second base and he was pretty apprehensive about it. 'Ummms' and 'aaaahs' were being uttered in abundance.

And then the reality check – the guy on our screen finally penetrated the girl, after toying around with his junk and saying 'trust me' on a loop.

"Yikes, there's blood on his, uhmm, on his, yeah, umm, I can't watch that."

"You're a pussy or what? Those drops of blood were enough to freak you out? What about the rivers of blood we handle every frigging month?"

"*Shi*. I can't do this. We're fine till foreplay and making out."

"No, let's do this."

Amar thought for a while and had a eureka moment, "I don't have a condom. Phew! No unsafe sex."

His face turned pale when I took out a condom from my back pocket and waved it at his face.

"You aren't going anywhere tonight. I shall take your virginity," I declared.

Oh boy, was he shit scared! And adorable as always!

All that drama was taking place after we had gotten drunk on music in the Weekender extravaganza. There was this Bangla rock band called 'Fossils'. I didn't get a single word while they played, but their music had a zing. And the dude Dadlani brought on a sufi rock dedication to Nusrat Fateh Ali Khan's songs. Last in line was the maestro himself. A.R. Rehman was in town and no guesses there, he made our evening worth all the head bangs in the air and the following neck pain.

While en route to Amar's room, I asked him, "Music is pure love. What kind of a love story do you want?"

"Like us, maybe? Isn't ours one?"

"Are we in love?"

"If you were, you wouldn't have asked that question."

I felt kinda stupid then, but continued, "Do you ever feel that you have settled for me?"

"Again, you wouldn't be on my bike right now and my company for the Weekender, if that was the case. There will be always someone smarter than you, prettier than you, deeper than you and perhaps sweeter than you. There's no end if we keep on searching. Now you make me laugh, dance with me during the *visarjan*, smart enough to shut people up and the kid in you is still furiously alive. I have no complaints. We're never too good for someone. You think, I'm outta your league, while I feel the same for you, on an intellectual level. But how does it matter if we feel the music together? If the same little things bring joy to our hearts, how does it matter?"

"That was something, honey. Don't stop there, finish it off with a quote to remember."

"Well, Nafisa, I'm an ordinary guy with an ordinary life who believes in and wishes for an extraordinary love. Can you give me that?"

I didn't have an answer for him, but I hugged him tighter and let the silence provide my answer. He understood and was probably even hurt. But I didn't know the answer. When is one sure that it's love? I had no idea. And I could not say yes to an extraordinary love request with a confused yes. I had to be sure.

To make the awkward pause disappear, I changed the topic, "How about I say thank you to you tonight?"

"Okay, umm, how exactly?"

"Let's have sex."

And he abruptly braked his bike to an absolute halt.

"I don't think I'm ready for it," Amar said.

"You just stole my line there."

"Really? You seriously want to do it tonight?"

"Yes. Screw me like a bitch. Make crazy sexy love to me tonight."

He had expressions of an engineer who was supposed to write an answer for sixteen marks when all he knew was the one-liner definition of the topic. Well, he could not gather the courage to penetrate me that night and yet penetrated me in a way only he could. I had to begin the introspection. Why was I not sure of our *Amar prem*? What was holding me back?

7

It had been three weekends that I had been ditching home. Amar kept me and my sexual hormones engaged, you know. Sorta the honeymoon phase of our furiously short and sexy relationship. So on the fourth weekend of the month, I decided it was time to give a break to them tired libidos.

Boarded our sucker PMT bus and the seat was hot enough to cook my arse to an omelette. I arrived unannounced on the door with nothing but a sweat-loaded face and hair.

"*Tu*?" Mumma said, surprised.

"*Haan, mera bhi ghar hai*," I said and leaned for a big hug.

Mumma stepped back, saying, "Go to the bathroom. I'm not hugging this sweaty monster."

"I hate you, you beautiful non-sweaty mumma with those perfect braids."

As I threw my bag and shoes to unknown destinations, I asked, "How come I got curly hair? I mean, they are neither Kangana curly nor Tamanna straight, somewhere in the middle of that spectrum where it just sucks. No braid, no ponytails for me, ever. Only loose hair and a prayer for mother nature to blow some wind."

"*Ye duniya agar mil bhi jaaye to kya hai*?" Poet mumma rhetorized, before going back to the kitchen.

I had a bath and slipped into a comfortable night suit.

"Where's papa?"

"Left for office for an urgent issue."

"*Saale bhen*… don't even spare him on weekends."

"A!" Mumma raised her voice, extending her mono-syllable scold word.

"Sorry."

"Hmm. It's a hectic project, he can't help it."

"Hmm. So what are you cooking for me?"

She pointed to the *chhole* and in went the *tadka*. Oh, the smell of *mummy ke haath ka tadka*! I directed the outgoing steam to my nostrils with both palms and breathed heaven in.

"Hungry *na*?"

"Yes, very. *Lavkar banao* mumma."

I got back to sexting in the meantime.

I texted: *What's poor little soldier doing?*

He texted: *Lying down, all sad, with no caves to explore today.*

Me: *Make him go up and down na. Lend him a hand.*

He: *He's used to a softer hand these days.*

Me: *Cave is missing her explorer.*

He: *Tongue is busy right now, having an affair with beer.*

Me: *Oh yeah? My lips wanna have an affair with yours and bite them skin off.*

He: *My lips wanna suck something right now. Wonder where are my two melons?*

Me: *Right under my palms. Ladies can grope them itty-bitty-titties anytime they want.*

He: *And that fat, not at all curvy belly?*

Me: *Is waiting to pounce on chhola-bhatura and add some more fat to rub your face in. I miss my biscuits, dude.*

He: *Guys can feel them up anytime they want, if they got one or rather six as the fad goes.*

Me: *God, it was so hot this morning, got all sweaty when I reached home.*

He: *I wanna make you hot and sweaty right now from a completely different source of heat.*

Me: *Oh kiss me dammit. Just kiss me.*

"Ready, Nafisa. I have served you, come eat."

Me: *Gotta eat. Okay bye.*

He: *Yeah, I'll fantasize now and do some exercise. Bye.*

So I gobbled up an apparent endless supply of *bhaturas* till my tummy screamed for mercy. *Ghar ka khaana* is pure bliss. I burped once midway and mumma asked, "Done?"

"No way," I told her, "keep them coming."

As I struggled to wipe off the last trace of gravy and couple of last *chhole* pieces from my plate, I realized my tummy could explode any minute then. I licked clean all five fingers and the plate looked as good as washed anew.

"You better go for a walk, beta," Mumma chuckled and teased me, "you look kind of pregnant right now."

"Maaaawm," I raised my voice, extending my mono-syllable word.

"Just joking, *beta*. For a mother, her children are never too full. Go rest."

So I lay down in my room uttering 'ufff' every alternate time I exhaled. And then began the acute pain in my stomach. I was moaning in pain soon enough.

Mumma came and checked on me, "What happened?"

"I think it's an infection. I know my body, mumma. I'm an adult woman now."

"Haha, very funny. It's just gas. I think you overate."

"I know what gas pain is, but this is unbearable, mumma. Give me an antibiotic, please."

"No. I'll look for something to soothe your pain, wait."

"Not those minty green pearls, mumma."

She was looking for the green liquid that rhymes with 'Putin Zara' that had turned into cute little green pearls over the course of time, but I hated to consume them. They were eye-candy for me, never actually a medicine. It felt cruel to eat them.

"Seems we have none at home. I'll go buy some, wait."

That was the last time I talked to her. There was a pharmacy adjacent to our society. A ten-minute affair at max. But half an hour had already passed when I began to wonder. And then I got the fateful call.

"Hello, hello? Yeah, whoever this is, the lady with this phone was hit by a speeding car. We called ambulance but…"

"But what?" I asked, my hands trembling, barely able to hold the phone.

"She is dead already."

"No no no no no!" I blabbered, struck by fear and horror unbeknownst to me till that moment.

"Shit shit shit shit shit shit, oh god, no no no no no no," I kept uttering, hitting the lift keys to make it go down faster, never realizing when the abdomen pain stopped registering itself and how I felt only terror.

I was running and running, tears awash all over my face. There was a large herd gathered around the pharmacy.

"No no!" I uttered again, hands on my knees, panting and wishing that it was some other lady. I took steps unwillingly and made way through the crowd.

And there lay my beautiful non-sweaty mumma with those perfect braids, bathed in blood with a smashed face. Dead.

8

I didn't cry when she was taken to the hospital, brought back home and put up on display in whites for people to pay homage to. I sat beside her toe all that time, tugging at it and hoping that it was all a bad dream and I would be soon woken up by mumma only to be given a lovely good morning kiss on my cheek.

I guess life is just one big bad dream. You wake up when you die. And if it's not bad enough yet, just wait for it, because life spares nobody.

Theory of relativity was on display shamelessly, time passing as if it was bribed to go ultra-slow. Never happened during the late night love calls from the terrace – nights ran past me as if they had a train to catch.

Papa had not spoken a word. I was puzzled, rather frightened, imagining the kind of turmoil tugging at his heart. Get called to the office, daughter comes unannounced and wife dies on the same lazy afternoon, trying to buy a stupid green medicine – perfect ingredients for the shittiest weekend of one's life.

I didn't cry when she was covered with all that wood from the precious trees we wish to save. The same fire that had cooked chhole-bhature for us was going to cook her up. I had to dollop *shuddha desi ghee* all around the wood to aid the fire in burning her entirely. Papa was still mum and I was handed over the torch to light up mumma. And I set her on fire. Half an hour later, mumma was no more. Only remained a heap of dusty ash.

People were expecting papa to gather the ash in a pretty container and take it back home to give a memorable farewell to ash mumma in one of them sacred scenic rivers. But he walked up, gathered the ash in a bucket hastily, walked calmly over and threw the ash down a steep drain that led to a gutter. There were few bones still recognizable and considerably larger in size. Papa filled the bucket with water and splashed them down the drain. And my ash mumma disappeared in the black gutter water. Not much differentiates a Ganga from gutter when death has pissed you off. Not a word from him still.

We came back home and none of us was hungry for dinner. I went to my room and closed the door shut, lying on my bed with still darkness and haunting silence as company. And soon enough, crockery was crashing to pieces, utensils were being thrown and glass was being shattered. Papa had either gone berserk or returned to reality finally. I couldn't really tell. I curled up and realized that mumma had indeed died. All her hugs, kisses and laughter came flashing into my mind. And I cried. I cried my guts out, screaming in silence.

◆

"Mumma, close the curtains *na*. Can't sleep with the sunlight in my face."

I rubbed my eyes and looked around, only to realize that mumma was no more. It was as if my heart was stabbed by a dagger all over again when it was already dead, beating just for the heck of it.

I was thinking that the death and following funeral was the storm that we had endured, but the real storm is what ensues after the funeral. You get rid of the body, but the absence continues to haunt you forever.

Nobody to wake me up, nobody to make me breakfast, nobody to give a morning hug to, nobody to argue with over my inverted sleep cycle, nobody to give me late night hair-oil *champi*, nobody to discuss *aam aurat* problems and nobody to close curtains as well.

I couldn't sleep anymore. I got up and saw papa making tea for himself. Umm, I could have gone helped him, but I still don't know how to cook anything other than the most (in)famous noodle brand of our nation and literally the staple food of us hostelites.

How was he going to deal with it? I had only lost my mother. He had lost his wife and the mother of his baby. It's unbearable to think of losing your partner and living without them. Should we never love to avoid the pain? No, that would be foolish. I guess it's cruel to ask your better half, the mate of your soul to go on without you. If one dies, other should die too. Lovers should die together, yes. Excluding the suicidal ones of course, for they already follow the trend.

A home really comes to a grinding halt without a mother. There's no pressure cooker *seeti* whistling, no haggling over *kaamwali bai ka pagaar*, no yoga channels whose exercises were poorly imitated, the garbage still waiting to be disposed off and those little art antiques and our souls left to gather dust of this world.

Papa made his tea in the meantime and sat on the sofa, his hand confused whether to opt for the TV remote or newspaper. I just stood there looking at him.

He turned to me and braved a genuine smile.

"Oh, you're up. Tea? I'll make another cup?" he asked.

I tried not to cry but a couple of tears trickled down my cheek. I looked at my wifeless papa, trying to assure me with his smile which was soon failed by a stream of that salty goddamned liquid.

I hugged him and asked, "How will we make it without her? Did I kill her, papa?"

"You'll never again curse yourself for her death. Just remember that she's still watching us. Only surviving won't do. I want you to live, beta. Promise me that you'll live your life and make the most of it. No regrets, okay?"

"Hmm. Promise, papa. I promise."

And we both broke down, crying profusely, while mumma's spirit watched us. The storm had just begun.

◆

I had not known a feeling of terror greater than that, ever. My heart was pounding as if it had just escaped a murder attempt. But that feeling was something else. As if there was a huge hollow space beneath my chest and I could feel it growing. I couldn't stop staring at the ground below. I walked baby steps and wished that they start taking me backwards, somewhere secluded, where I could just sit down and cry and cry. I walked up a couple of floors with my neck hung down and faced the moment of truth.

My batch-mates who were laughing, hastily copying assignments to submit, bitching, just talking, gave up all of it and decided to stare at me. Damn! I knew they didn't do it intentionally, but all of them had this intensely pitiful looks on their faces and their eyes reeked of sympathy enough to bring about world peace. It made matters worse for me. I couldn't move ahead then. To be honest, I wanted a hug really really bad.

And the bloody, bloody heart wanted to pop outta my body. I wanted to run away, but my roll call was near enough.

"Hey, I'm sorry about your mother. Be strong. Don't look so sad."

As soon as I managed a smile to assure her, another girl commented, "Look at her, she's smiling already. Disgusting. How can she?"

Are you fucking kidding me? People do judge you and you're never good enough for all of them. The emptiness only grew on hearing that. I shouldn't have smiled, I concluded.

That's when someone tapped on my shoulder. I turned around to get a tight hug. It was Pia. And my eyes immediately got swamped with tears. I tried hard to keep it in though. Didn't want to create a scene at college and come across as a miserably weak girl. Last thing I wanted was any more attention on me. I was doing that myself, scarily well. Never had I felt so self-conscious before.

God, I missed mumma.

"Shh, it's okay," Pia said, hugging me tighter.

That was the moment I realized that the world hadn't stopped existing. And I had to face all of it, with all its beauty and cruelty, alone. By myself.

Pia's top was getting soaked with my tears as she kept repeating, "Shh, it's okay."

And I kept whispering between my sobs to her, "No. No, it isn't."

9

Fuck me. Fuck me for not going for another naughty weekend with Amar. Fuck me for deciding to go home. Fuck me for not even calling one of my parents. Fuck me for gorging on mumma's chhole-bhatura like I was starving for ages. Fuck me for not stopping when I had burped midway. Fuck me for not going for a walk after lunch. Fuck me for confusing stupid gas with a food infection. Fuck me for trying to be an adult with that antibiotic shit. Fuck me for having complained at all. Fuck me for not going out to buy the goddamned medicine myself. Fuck me for killing mumma. Fuck me. Fuck!

I was trapped in the vicious regret cycle again. I had promised papa not to blame myself for her death, but I simply couldn't escape the thought that I was the one who triggered the butterfly effect. A single different reaction and mumma would have been alive. Something, man, something that could have turned it around.

The feeling intensified whenever I sat alone on the footpath of Vidyapeeth. Existence becomes a wicked exercise for loners like us. We can't endure people, so we keep to ourselves. But how does one endure the devil within that eats us inch by inch, devouring every bite of our soul and injecting it with infinite guilt? The peak of self-loathing, no doubt about that.

Amar? Yeah, I had cut him off. He did arrive unannounced a week after mumma's demise. And that brought ugly remnants yet again, so his surprise trick had backfired even before I walked out to meet him. Our conversation didn't last too long either:

"Hey, how are you holding up?"

I just gave him the awkward smile face and hugged him.

"Well, I don't really know what to say. Can't even say that I understand. Umm, I haven't lost anyone that I love. To death, I mean."

"It's okay," I said, patting his back, as he patted back mine.

Our eyes could not gather the courage to look into each other. I don't know what it was – hopelessness, pain or just plain tears. But we simply could not. He decided it was best that he left me to myself. I needed a break from his presence. There was hardly any dull moment when we were together. Our relationship was riding at breakneck speed and that was the moment of truth for us. Absolute screeching halt. Apparently, nobody had a clue how to go about it. It was the exam we hadn't prepared for.

And I simply could not make peace with the fact that a great wife and caring mother was taken away instead of the horny, mostly drunk and pretentious teeny adult failing miserably at growing up.

A couple of classmates who noticed me sitting all alone, with their concerned eyes, asked, "Hey, all okay *na*? Sitting alone?"

Frankly, I was staring at nothing, into a sort of void. I don't even remember the expression on my face. I smiled awkwardly I guess and didn't even utter a word. Just moved my neck in all directions, hoping to convey it was all fine. I lied, they understood I lied and everyone decided to let it be.

Trance. That would be the word to describe the feeling on those nights.

Except that trance was nothing like the gift of weed. I was pushed off the cliff into an endless merciless abyss, with grief consuming me like them chhole-bhatura.

How was I supposed to win the battle? It was me vs me.

10

There are times when I can't hold it in. The break-down happens once every two-three days. It's a slow poison. You can feel the poison running through your veins and corrupting your smile. Once the poison enters your system, you never laugh genuinely. It's fake. You know it when you smile. And what kills you within is that nobody catches your lie. You have deceived them. Each one of them. Friends tell you, you are the sunshine. Always a smile adorns your face. How I wish I could scream to all of them – don't believe the person who always smiles.

I long to cry. And I know people would lend me a shoulder for it. But I can't. I pretend to go for a walk, find an isolated place and let my eyes cry. This is my natural response. This is what I feel since she died. I'm not always smiling, I'm crying within. How I wish someone could see through me to see these tears! I let my defence fall for these brief moments. The next morning, I rebuild my emotional wall to block every memory of hers. I can't afford to remember her. That's the only way I can survive and not end up killing myself.

After a while, people move on. While you realize that you're still stuck in the past. The world stops spinning for you. They continue dealing with their shitty relationships, cribbing about lack of money, ranting about improving the education system and jerking off to porn to call it a day. For a week, and if you're lucky, for a month, everyone will ask if you're fine. What about the torment that follows after the week, after the month? Who will ask me then?

So I turned to anonymity. Poured my heart out over the internet. Told strangers how vulnerable I had become, how badly I wanted to hear the right words, how senseless this life had become. Fact is, nobody cares that your mother died, nobody gives a damn that you're hungry for some love, nobody could possibly understand unless they've lost someone – the one person who mattered the most. Are they to blame then? Or me to expect it?

I opened up my soul to anyone and everyone. Few guys tried to hit on me, few wanted to fuck me right away, while rest of them didn't even respond. Girls had consoling words to offer to me, but not their precious time. Few of them were really supportive, but they talked when they wanted to. What about the night that I need to endure? Who's willing to listen to me?

'I'm ready to beg, if you want. But please hear me out.'

Yes, that's me when I say hi to you.

And when people don't respond the way I want them to, agony accumulates and pumps in more poison in my system. It makes me angry, makes my blood boil. It's directed at them as well as me. Why can't I be happy again? Why don't I smile genuinely, for once? Am I this pathetic? And in the midst of this chaos, I murmur an answer within that pacifies my burning rage – I'll see how you deal with it when your lifeline will be cut off.

PS: If only she was here, I wouldn't be writing to you as well.

Nafisa

◆

Later the same night, after writing the letter, I texted Amar- *Breakdown alert.*

He texted back- *I'll pick you up at 10.*

So I wore a t-shirt with a quote from that famous nerdy sitcom rhyming with 'Duh pig rang fury'. And no points for guessing, the quote was of the annoyingly genius, cute and funny guy who runs the show almost single-handedly. Coupled that with jeans and a hoodie. Not exactly a club outfit, but then those one-piece dresses have never been up my alley. As a drastic consequence of that, I don't have a new pouting DP to showcase every other weekend with them shiny sunglasses, bright lipsticks and a one-piece, teasing guys with a glimpse of cleavage. Yeah, poor me! (psst… sarcasm)

While engulfed in those thoughts, Amar arrived on his bike whose name rhymed with 'ulcer'. I became the pillion rider and he drove off, me hugging him tight as fuck.

I remembered my promise – "I'll hug you so tight, will never let you go."

And I let my tears have their way. Each sob making me hug him tighter. My head rested comfortably on his shoulder and it seemed the safest place in the world. He caressed my hands whenever we halted at a signal, sang for me the lullaby, 'Don't you worry, don't you worry, child. See, heaven's got a plan for you'.

Sentimentally, it was the right song to sing, but I knew in my heart that the universe doesn't give a fuck about any of us. Anyway, I let him sing, my sweetheart.

As he parked the bike, I stood with my shoulders stooping low, to the ground almost. He wiped my tears, chuckled, ran his fingers through my curly hair to arrange them and cheek-kissed me.

"You look beautiful, now lemme see that dimple of yours," he said, making me smile like only he could and we headed to our favourite dance floor destination Penthouze.

We gulped down beers till my head began spinning, feet became wobbly and regret cells were numbed down. I stood up and announced that I wanted to dance, as I fell on the floor ass-first. The DJ there usually experiments a lot with music, but since I liked that trance piece of club dancing from the genius soundtrack of the movie wherein a lame guy gets his heart broken by a fake Kashmiri, eats samosas to recover from the pain and ends up becoming a torn mad famous musician, Amar begged the DJ to play it for me. Well, the song wasn't played, but then, my boyfriend tried at least. It's difficult to convince a DJ to play a song for a drunk panda on the floor with a hoodie.

He came back and apologized. Man, it was such an 'awww' moment for me. I pulled him close and kissed him and kissed him till the music faded in my ears and all I felt were his lips and the beer-charged saliva. I had survived another night of breakdown.

11

A month had passed and I was trying to bury mumma's memories. Got a call from papa on a weekend asking me to come over.

So I went to the mumma-less home and found that papa was busy packing boxes with her stuff.

"Are we packing all of it away?" I asked him.

"Yes."

"Umm, why?"

"I can't bear to see them. I tried, but I can't."

I nodded an 'I understand'.

"So I needed some help with it. Thought I would call you home. How are *you* by the way?"

I nodded a 'No, not fine', compressing my lips, squinting my eyes a little to create the expression 'I'm trying though'.

He nodded an 'I understand'.

Papa handed over mumma's framed death photo for packing and I dropped a tear on the glass frame. My beautiful mumma, Tamanna, with those black eyes, slender eyebrows, a black *bindi*, braided black hair and a smile that could end world wars. There is an unusually enigmatic feminine aura about ladies from the one up generation. Simplicity is beautiful. Mumma had no make-up on and still looked like a million dollars. And all that eventually became her death photo. The glass frame had a small pool of tears by then. But I packed it away.

"Bring all the saaris and salwars from the cupboard. I'll donate them."

"Umm..."

I was pondering if I would ever slim down to fit in them. Then I realized, I would have to run or go on a diet for that to happen. No surprises there, I followed the order and went to collect them.

I was just about done emptying the cupboard, when I found a diary sitting comfortably under mumma's favorite red salwar. I punched the salwars and saaris to fit them inside the box, closed the flaps, taped it and examined the diary again.

Green colored cover. Year 1991. Smudged black ink on the cover, titled- MAGIC.

I flipped it open and saw the first diary entry. It was mumma's handwriting. I was smiling again, wiping away my tears of joy.

◆

So there I was, smiling like a silly girl, while staring at a diary for a change, not our usual screens. Papa was still busy packing and I couldn't contain my excitement. So I opened the diary, smelled the pages, uttered a long sigh of pleasure and started reading the first entry:

'Chase your dreams.'

'Make it big.'

I wonder if such statements apply for girls like me. For girls who can't escape their inevitable fate of an arranged marriage. I can't think of a single act of my life whose ultimate goal has not been marriage.

"Enroll her for a graduation course. Graduate girls can be married off easily."

"Teach her cooking and to make round rotis. The way to a man's heart is through his stomach."

"It's time she starts dressing like a woman and acting like one. She'll soon get married."

Nobody asked which course I wanted to choose for my graduation.

"Oh, it doesn't matter. Any course will do. We need the degree certificate, that's it."

So here I am, pursuing stupid commerce, when I wanted to go for literature.

Nobody asked me if I like cooking. The fact that a girl might hate cooking is an alien thought for Aai and the auntijis. I'm quite lazy, to be honest. But a girl doesn't have the luxury of being lazy in India. Sad but true.

And what's with this word 'woman' anyway?

Girl – immature, inelegant, careless, ugly.

Woman – goddess, beautiful, graceful, mature.

I don't agree. The only separator is age. Girls are young, women are older. Period.

Girls like me are doomed. And the worst part is it's our parents who let us down. Not much to blame then because they can play the emotional blackmail card anytime. They have raised you, so you owe it to them to marry a person of their liking.

It might be rude to say this but such people should never become parents in the first place. This is not called raising a daughter. I'm more of a circus animal who's being trained to excel at marriage.

I'll make sure my daughter won't be.

◆

Wow! I mean, wow! I was blown away. I sat in disbelief. I had fallen in love with that entry. Mumma could write and how. Wow! I mean, wow! I was charmed by the honest confessions in that entry. It was plain truth, delivered without any sugar-coating. Sober realities that stung. Mumma was resisting marriage while she was still graduating.

It must have been a looming thought, rather a looming judgment. I *toh* shudder to even think of marriage. Poor mumma of mine. I peeked out the door to see that papa had sat down for a breather, eyes closed, face facing the ceiling. So I turned the page, smelled it again and began reading-

Diary, meet my friend, Ghazal. She's the reason I'm writing right now. One who has the same complaints about life makes for a great friend and bitching partner.

She is my vent but there have been times when I simply could not reveal it all. She understood and said, "Start keeping a diary and write whatever bothers you. If not me, tell her at least and vent it out."

"Vent?" I asked.

"Outlet. An outlet for your suppressed strong emotions."

"Ah, I see."

Yeah, so we were walking towards our bus-stop, when a girl on a Bajaj Sunny whizzed past us. And did her hair look stunning! I couldn't move for a moment. Ghazal stood frozen as well, but her usual smile had vanished.

She opened up in the bus.

"I want to ride a bike."

"Okay...and?"

"I want to ride a bike sans burqa."

"Sans?"

"Without."

"Oh!"

She was staring at nothing, lost in thought while I was short of words.

"A woman riding a bike signifies liberty, freedom and power for me. I want to feel the air in my hair. Let them loose and see them fly with the wind. A ride without a burqa, that's it. And I think, I'll die a happy soul then."

Her words hit me hard. Such a simple wish and yet it seems impossible. How trivial it is for the rest of us, I wondered. She left at her stop and we didn't exchange any words. No customary goodbye wave as well.

Perhaps she's venting it right now in her diary. I promise you that bike ride, Ghazal. I'll make it happen.

I owe it to her. Don't I, diary?

◆

Okay, that had left a melancholic taste in my mouth. It had never ever occurred to me that riding a bike was such a luxury. But I guess, that's how the world works. We have a lot for being thankful, but *yeh dil always maange more*. And mumma called Ghazal her bitching partner there. I was pleasantly shocked. I mean, it was hard for me to imagine her using cuss words.

"Are you done with the cupboard, beta?" Papa asked and disturbed the field of the magnetic hypnotic charm of mumma's diary.

I put the diary in my college bag and walked out with the box of mumma's clothes. Mumma's belongings were being disposed of, but the one I had discovered was going to prove far more enduring. Tamanna was still alive in those pages of 1991. Still very much alive.

12

February had arrived and I was in no mood to head out, no, not even with myself. It was becoming more and more difficult to handle my own thoughts. Alone time brought a tsunami of guilt with it. So I decided to attend college, remain among people for as long as I could, read one entry from mumma's diary, plug in some music after that and just pray that I would fall asleep without crying.

And mumma being the perfect mother that she was, she had written just the entry I needed in February:

It's the most depressing day of the year, diary. Valentine's day. I hate going out on this day just to realize how sad my life is. But Ghazal had other plans. She is one... what you call it... let me check a dictionary wait, it starts with 'en'... I remember that much.

Yeah, she's an enigma, diary. She really is. I wonder, why she is doing this commerce course when she is so good with words. Anyway, she wanted us to bunk our classes and go to Saras Baug aka lover's park.

I saw couples as far as my eyes could reach.

"See all these couples coupling around, honey. You think they're happier than you are? Let's find ourselves a nice seat. The show is about to start."

I had no idea what Ghazal was talking about.

'Jai hanumaan, jai hanumaan, jai shree ram, jai shree ram'

We could hear the slogans being shouted and the sound was approaching closer with each passing moment.

Ghazal squeezed my hand and said, "Oh, you'll thank me for this, Tammy. Wait and watch."

Within a minute, an army of men dressed in white with saffron scarves came running in, holding hockey sticks, bamboo sticks, just sticks. They began slapping and hitting every couple they could catch. It felt like a riot. A riot on the day of love.

And I loved these men for beating up the coupling couples. I hate the fact that while I'm single and destined for an arranged marriage, the rest of the world is busy having a girlfriend/boyfriend. Girls were being slapped, boys were being beaten.

"Yeah, hit them harder. Valentine day sucks, yes. Jai shree ram. Jai hanumaan."

I couldn't stop cheering for those men. Ghazal told me that it was not evil to enjoy the proceedings.

She precisely said, "These are the simple joys of life. What I don't have, what I can't have, why should they have it? These men in white believe in equality and are working to making single people like us happy. We should thank them for this noble deed."

Boys were forcibly asked to hold their ears and say sorry to India's culture and traditions. Girls were asked to tie raakhis to their boyfriends.

"Promise us that you will treat her as your sister and respect our heritage. We won't let these bloody western traditions ruin our Mother India!"

And they hit the guys' bums again, in case they didn't nod immediately.

Haha, I still can't stop laughing. Best Valentine's Day ever. No regrets about being single, diary. No regrets.

◆

I swear, I hadn't laughed *that* hard in months. God, my cruel cruel mumma and her kick-ass friend Ghazal! I wish I had a bestie like her. No regrets though. I had Tamanna's diary. I love you, mumma.

13

It was yet another lousy uninspiring day of college when a little storm arrived on paper. It was Kiaan's letter. His first reply, that read:

THE DILEMMA OF UNREQUITED LOVE

So you see them and you're struck by lightning. A wave of goosebumps goes on a rampage. It dawns upon you that your heart is indeed pumping blood into your veins; breathing becomes a conscious process, and you realize that the fabled thing called 'being alive' does exist. Practical people call it infatuation. Mad ones like me have already fallen into the trap.

No, it wasn't love at first sight. I had seen her many a times. If beauty alone triggers the process for you, then you're just being shallow. It's for the world to see if she's a stunner, that's obvious. Where's the fun in pointing out the obvious for her? It was when I fell in love with her naked soul. We couldn't stop talking; our conversations ranging from the philosophy of existence to the autotuned songs.

Nights and nights went by and words flowed perpetually. There was never a dull moment, the peak of my own happiness scared me at times and she's the one to tell you that there's a word for it – cherophobia. The last person you think of before sleeping has your heart. And she's become the one. You close eyes with her name on your lips and you wake up to utter her name again. You're absolutely, utterly, positively smitten with her. Love is the new black.

You look at her again when you meet and she doesn't look the same anymore. Yes, she was pretty. Anyway, that was obvious, but you look at her and notice that her canine tooth is never visible when she smiles. It's a goofy bunny smile but she's still a stunner; you observe the intricacies of her eyes. Oh, the universe in her eyes – the way they light up when she talks of books, her latest favorite nail paint shade, graffiti, the dress she bought from a sale at a bargained price. And how words have an identity of their own – she tells you that gorgeous is when you can't resist mouthing a 'wow' and beautiful is when your admiring gaze is enough. Her hair's all messy, far from the perfectly straight and bouncy ones they show you in conditioner ads, but a strand flirts with her eyes time and again and you wish the struggle continues. You notice how she speaks at a tone lower than yours always. While you're ecstatic at the sight of her, almost screaming, when you hear her tone again and it soothes you like those chirping birds. Now you know the real her. A stunner for the shallow world, a real stunner for you. This is the moment when your idea of her and the reality make love to each other. And the next time you see her is the moment they call love at first sight.

Finally, guts gather and love confesses itself. Your eyes can't lie anymore. She's a woman after all, evolved to identify the non-verbal hints, be it her year-old child or her latest unintentional victim. You talk again when you're back home and tell her that she seems perfect for you. Little do you know, the bubble is about to burst. She does love you but not in that way. And you're left in a state of disbelief. You read her statement again and scroll above, cherish those past joyous moments, scroll down and return to the disbelief. You wish to ask her the reasons, but then realize the futility of such questions. The ultimate judgment has been passed already. Make peace with that now. Somehow. Gosh, somehow!

And then the terrible loop begins. You're in love with her, she's not in love with you. She maintains a healthy conversation still, the spark still visible in her words, but yours starts dimming. And you wonder how she manages to do it. She says it's a guilt trip for her whenever she talks to you. So you try sounding alright, pretending to smile when she's around. You can't ruin it for her by admitting that you've become miserable. Still high on her, unmistakably. You decide whimsically to end all ties with her, to avoid her in college, stop talking altogether and try convincing yourself that it's possible. And the next moment, you're back to square one – you can't just lose someone so beautiful. It's pure horror for you – the thought that she would be gone from your life. You can't walk away nor can you persuade her into loving you. She just doesn't feel it for you. Intermittent moments of weakness nearly make you beg for a shred of her love. But she simply can't reciprocate. You lie down, trying to catch some sleep and solace, but with eyes wide open and a rotating fan staring back at you, it dawns on you that you're screwed as fuck. Fuck.

I'm sorry to hear about your mother, Nafisa.

Kiaan

◆

That fucker! How did he know about mumma? Oh okay, I had written a couple of Quora answers on it, I figured. Nevertheless, I was so pissed at him that my blood was not boiling, but had evaporated long ago. I was provoked enough to start writing the reply immediately.

Did you just compare unrequited love and death? Screw you, dude. I mean, I'm so disgusted right now that I won't waste anymore words. But screw you, man.

I have no idea what to write in this letter. I'm really low and angry these days. How to crawl outta it? People scare me now. I go for a walk and I feel everyone's watching me. I've become an instant sympathy inducing machine. And this Bharati Vidyapeeth backyard is so closely-knit with our college students, it's impossible to avoid them when I go for dinner. Maybe I'll ask for a mess dabba hereafter.

Anyway, tell me more about you. What makes you feel alive? For me, it used to be beer, sleep, ice-creams and seeing someone smile because of me. Well, now, I hardly look up. I can't make eye contact. Vulnerable is the word, I guess. My heart's a complete mess, that's the plain truth.

*I realize now that there's a downside to letters as well. We can't divert the conversation nor suggest anything to keep it going. And sending a letter with only this much doesn't seem worth it. Emails have much more swag. Play with colours, fonts, emojis and I save a tree as well *lazy good karma brownie points, yay**

Penmanship is declining, ain't it? We've become serial scrollers. Kinda killed off the art of handwritten letters. Agreed that the game-changer reading tab from the 'Aur dikhao, aur dikhao' fame is far more convenient, but a screen can never replace the smell of paper. Whatcha say?

Oh wait, I just wrote down your school of thought there, right? Pardon my faulty memory.

Anyway, come to think of it, I remember a Stan Lee meme:

When asked if online comics would replace actual books, Stan Lee said: "Comics are like boobs. They look great on a computer, but I'd rather hold one in my hand."

Epic, right?

I can open my heart to you. You're a total stranger to me and this letter's the best outlet. I think, a tree can die right now; I wanna save my soul first. Don't judge me, yeah? Sorry if I was rude in the first one. I'm a delight otherwise. I miss my mumma, Kiaan.

Love,

Nafisa

◆

And that's what you call mood swings. I was infuriated when I had gotten down to write the letter and within a paragraph, it had changed from anger to a soft confession to a polite ice-breaker to personally sponsored weird shit to acceptance to another soft confession. I fed the letterbox in our college and walked back to spend the night with the next diary entry.

14

What an interesting day, diary! Blood, letters, acid and marriages. I can't wait to tell you about it.

So I was walking out from college when a guy called me. It was Milind.

"Can I talk to you for a while, in private?"

"Umm… okay," I said.

He handed me a letter then. The content was all in red. At first glance, I just read ahead and ignored it. But I looked closely again and it didn't seem anything like the red ink my teachers used.

I was quite scared by then and asked him, "What is it written with?"

"It's my blood, Tamanna," he answered proudly.

I didn't know what to say, diary. I just kept reading.

He had written every little detail about me. The fact that I applied kohl only on Fridays, the blue salwar that was reserved for boring Mondays, playing with my hair whenever I got nervous in a test, giggling with my mouth covered by a palm, etc. It was astonishing. I could have never guessed someone was observing me so closely.

His letter ended with a little shayari that I still remember. Yes, it was that beautiful:

Patta patta boota boota haal humara jaane hai,

jaane najaane gul hi najaane, baag to saara jaane hai.

"Wow, who wrote this poem?"

"I did."

I was more impressed than scared at that time. He seemed to be a great poet. He broke my thoughts by saying, "I'm in love with you, Tamanna. Can we marry?"

"What? But we're talking for the first time today. How… how can… marry?!"

He held my hand and kept saying 'Please', over and over again. I didn't know how to react, he touched me just like that. That was… out… it was… something out… umm, I can't remember the word, wait. Ghazal was shouting that word till she got off at her stop. Let me check the dictionary.

Outrageous. Finally found it, hush!

That was the same time when Ghazal spotted me and came running. She held his hand and kept saying "Hadd, hadd, back off" over and over again.

"What's happening over here?" Ghazal asked.

I handed her the letter and she realized immediately that it was blood. I could tell from her eyes.

She pulled me further from him.

In favour of Milind though, I told Ghazal, "The poetry at the end was written by him, isn't it great?"

"What is your reaction to all this nonsense?"

She looked all serious, angry and tense.

"He cut himself to write me a letter. I feel kind of sorry for him. I'll think about giving him a chance."

"That's all he wants?"

"Well, he wants us to marry."

"Chyaaaichi…wait, I'll talk to him. You don't dare say a word!"

Ghazal stood face to face with him and asked, "You love Tamanna, hmm?"

He nodded eagerly.

"And what if she says no?"

"Huh?"

"What if she doesn't want to marry you? Doesn't want to see you ever?"

"She can't, I mean, she... she won't. I love her truly."

"Oh really, do you? Won't you throw acid on her if she refuses your crazy proposal? You're ready to cut yourself and spill blood just to talk to her. You're obsessed, this is not love. And you don't seem ready to accept a rejection. 'Yes' is the only answer you want."

I could see anger accumulating in Milind's eyes. Truth hit him hard, I think. He didn't speak a word.

Ghazal continued taking his class, "So let me tell you something, mister lover. If you even think of throwing acid on her face, I promise I'll bathe your body in acid. I'll kill you, I swear. Better stay away from her. Bloody liar!"

And she said, looking at me, "That poem was written by a legend – the Urdu poet Mir."

He ran off as if Ghazal was going to eat him alive the next moment. Her behaviour was quite outrageous for me. I could never shout at someone like that even if I tried.

As we walked together towards our bus stop, Ghazal said, "Outrageous, completely outrageous. Wants to marry and tries to lure you with Mir's poetry, that swine. You're innocent, honey. Don't let people take advantage of it. You can't love someone out of pity. Always remember that."

"What about that bathing him in acid part? Did you really mean it?"

"Well, no. But you got to go mad before they do. The one who gets scared loses the game. That's how you play."

I'm really wondering, who is more of a psycho – that guy or my Ghazal. Good night, diary.

◆

God, stalking has taken an altogether different form now. People follow you virtually and keep track of your whereabouts. And I still can't decide which one of them is creepier. But… umm, I guess, an internet bully is still manageable than a potential bloody psycho. Anyway, I had gone to the terrace for a walk after reading that. I paced up and down and felt the breeze in my hair. I hadn't had a blank mind, devoid of thoughts, since ages. Since I wasn't exactly sleepy either, I decided to cheat and read another diary entry that same night.

Today was dedicated to our discussion on arranged and love marriages, diary. We ended up bunking classes. Such was our frustration with arranged marriages that the conversation breaker was ultimately us going home.

It all started when I asked Ghazal this, while walking to the class, "What do you think of arranged marriages? I mean, I know we both hate it, but I want to talk about it."

Ghazal turned around instantly, "Yes, let's do this."

The sky was clear blue with no clouds in sight. The heat was kind of… ugh… something scotchy… dictionary, wait. Scorching heat, diary. That's what Ghazal said. But such was our frustration that we decided to bear it and just talk.

"Arranged marriage is like investing in a lottery, that game of gambling you hate, the rumoured betting they say that exists in cricket. It's all based on chance. I hate it when I'm not in control. I live twenty odd years only to let my parents decide what monkey I'm going to marry. And then, spend my life cooking for him, cleaning for him, adjusting to the whims of his stupid family, learning to cope with their rituals and fucking traditions – keep your head down, touch their feet, smile all along and get screwed between sheets."

"Calm down baba, it's okay. We're just discussing. You seem to be holding in more anger than me," I told Ghazal.

"See, it's kind of cute as well. Starting from scratch does seem interesting. Exploring someone you barely know, getting to know him, falling in love and making lovely looking babies. Hell or heaven for fifty years, all that depends on a fucking chance. I don't like that. My husband might treat me like a princess or his mother might burn me to death for dowry, who knows. This uncertainty scares me. I mean, I feel like one of those trained circus animals with my parents as the ringmaster. Even a lion jumps from one stand to another when tamed, but that's not its true nature. A lion is supposed to roar, free in the jungle. I never get to roar, neither before nor after the marriage. That's sad, Tammy."

"I agree. Love marriage is a risk you walk into. It's beautiful to find someone you can share your life with. Marriage is a big decision. It should be backed by concrete feelings for someone, not an intuition based on a formal meeting. Everyone acts like the purest and noblest human in an arranged marriage's parents' meeting. That isn't the whole truth. I do understand that a love marriage can fall apart as well. But it will be my decision and I will face it. I want that freedom of choice. We both are caged animals, yes."

"Arranged marriage makes love an obligation. In all reality, love should come first, marriage later, not the other way round. Just because our parents put up with all the shit doesn't mean I have to. Cultures change, Tammy. For next generations, love marriage won't be a war against parents, an act of rebellion against society or a lifetime achievement award for ourselves. We literally need to fight for our love. I really wish we don't have to."

"Amen to that."

"I have thought of my daughter's name already though – Nafisa. Love or arranged, that's not gonna change."

"Nafisa, huh? What does it mean?"

"Precious"

"And what if it's a boy?"

"Then I'll let that fucker decide, honey."

We laughed and laughed and then ordered another bowl of tarri to finish off our missal-paav and headed home. Nafisa is a beautiful name. What will I name my daughter, diary?

◆

Whoa whoa whoa! That's the origin story for my name, right there. People have been pestering me since forever as to why I have a Muslim-sounding name, if I'm not actually one. I ask them to bugger off and not judge people's religions from their names. I had never bothered to ask mumma either. I just loved my name so much. And I wondered about the generation gap and the seismic cultural shift. While we are still busy sharing the stories of our cruel exes, our mothers discussed marriages. What about Ghazal, though? Why didn't she ever visit mumma if they shared a bond like that? But I was already yawning and didn't want to cheat any more. So I decided not to kill the suspense and dozed off.

15

Every batch has its share of crazy teachers and crazier students to tackle them. The day started with the Mechanics lecture. This teacher spoke with a weird South-Indian accent, kept baring his rabbit teeth often and left for the parking that would be a town away wearing a the helmet, yes, he used to wear his helmet the moment he left the staffroom. And the morons that we were, every student marked proxy attendance for their bunch of friends. So, by the time the attendance sheet arrived at my desk, there were forty-five people present apparently, while the classroom only had sixteen mortal bodies occupying it. It was the first lecture in the morning and we expected our teacher to overlook that. Well, he did. The next were usual lectures where the teacher talks, nobody listens and is either busy sleeping, on phone or playing Bollywood hangman on paper. And like every alternate week, our principal paid us a *surprise* visit to ask questions that nobody could ever answer, mocked us and when his tummy was full with sadistic pleasure, left but only after claiming that he knew everything about everything.

Anyway, who gave a shit! I looked forward to only one thing and that night brought a revelation:

It was just another boring day in college, diary. Until Ghazal came up to me with a weird request.

"You need to meet this guy, Tammy," she told me.

"Who?" I asked.

"Jai"

"Who is he now?"

"Well, you can add one more to your list of admirers. Do you carry a lover magnet or what? I can bet those kohl-laden eyes kill the guys."

"Don't forget, I'm tall as well."

"Yeah yeah. You're just an extremely beautiful lady, that's all. Don't you act all vain now."

"Vain?"

"Showing an excessively high opinion of one's appearance."

"Ghazal, you deserve to act vain then. Aaishapath, I'll never be able to use words like those."

"Thanks, sweetheart. Now now, let's focus. So this guy, Jai, comes up to me and confesses that he would like to have a walk with you."

"And, you said?"

"The usual – get lost."

"But why a walk with me?"

"Who knows what his true intentions are. I'm not leaving you alone with a guy."

"So he just left?"

"No, damn it! That man has some nerves, I tell you. He tore a page from his diary, wrote a few lines with his ink pen and handed me over that page."

"Oh, okay. And said what?"

"Asked me to give this page and let you decide. Also, he did say that if you don't find that beautiful enough, you can throw it to the dustbin and he'll never again disturb you."

"Do you believe what he said?"

"Only time can tell. But he did look delicious Tammy. So, if that paper's content blows you away, I'll say you go ahead. He was holding a diary with him, perhaps his diary of poems. And a true poet won't misbehave with a lady."

"Why a poet? Any man shouldn't misbehave with a lady."

"Well, artists are a different breed, honey. Anyway, open na, that paper. And read it to me."

I won't lie, diary. It was one of the most beautiful things I have ever read. It was verbally as well as visually stunning. And I could not not meet him. I just had to see the man who had written that poem.

I met him today, diary. And he handed me his diary of poems to read. So we walked, while I kept reading. He didn't say a word. But he did smile before I left. He has an adorable smile, diary. And whenever he smiles, he blinks twice, rhythmically. It's really cute, rather delicious as Ghazal had said.

Oh, the poem? Here it is:

Dastak di hai maine, chalo tum bhi ab aaona,
Ho apni guftagoo, koi baat tum bhi bataona,
Chale jaana hai tumhein, to shikwa nahi dost,
Kaagaz kalam ki gustaakhi bus maaf kar jaana.

◆

Oh boy! Another infatuated guy, huh. But mumma did go for a walk with him. Hmm. And she wasn't complaining at all, rather sounded a bit inclined towards him. Jai, huh? Hmm.

16

Find what you love and let it kill you
—Bukowski

Who's the most badass woman in the world right now? Let's omit our mothers. I'll tell you about my latest discovery – Mathangi 'Maya' Arulpragasam aka M.I.A. Yeah, every artist's gotta be insane to be worth their salt, but this lady has rebel in her DNA, out and out. She is the only artist in history to be nominated for an Academy Award, a Grammy Award, a Brit Award, a Mercury Prize, and an Alternative Turner Prize.

And my god, she's turned forty this year and yet doesn't look a day older than twenty. Okay, maybe twenty-five, but I'm not exaggerating.

For me, she's right up there with John Lennon and Bob Marley, when she talks about world peace, multiculturalism and art being a medium to reflect the state of our society.

Maya was born in London but she had done her early schooling in Sri Lanka where, she recollects, students were sometimes sorted according to the hierarchy of their skin tone. So the fair skinned ones were in front and the darker ones filled up the back benches. Maya shared a seat with half-naked poor kids on the back benches. But she was the only one in the class who could draw and helped out other kids with illustrations whenever needed. And that's how she earned her way up the seating rank.

But then in mid-1980s, the civil war broke out and the Tamil minority found themselves in conflict. Non-English schools were being targeted and soldiers would put guns through holes in windows and shoot children. They had to learn to dive under the table or run to the neighbouring English-language school. This is when her father joined LTTE and she met him sporadically thereafter. She was ten when her family minus her father moved back to London.

And here's where the magic began. Maya had never had a formal exposure to the arts as a child. She was a young refugee in London, trying to cope with the new culture and unable to speak English. So she was taken outta the English or Science classes to paint for sets, make art or draw for plays. Her weapon was the colour riot she'd been a witness to in the so-called Third World. She'd grown next door to a textile factory that made and printed saaris.

Life turned around when she got into the best art school in London without having actually applied for it. She knew she wanted to study arts, but didn't have the grades to make it to CSM, London. So she began ranting up the head of the arts department, arguing she'd become a hooker if she didn't get in. She was told that sixteen thousand people apply for twenty seats, sit through six interviews and one couldn't just waltz in. Determined however, Maya wouldn't take no for an answer and was admitted eventually for her perseverance and chutzpah. Epic, right? Yeah, Stan Lee's reply was as well.

She studied film at CSM, but with the staggering talent she possessed, soon she ventured into graffiti-art, graphic design, designing her clothing and eventually broke into the music scene with the whackiest dance moves you'll ever watch in a music video – Galang. And a song that hip, beats sick as fuck still boasts of civil war references. You just watch her dance and tell me if she's not hypnotic.

And even her lyrics are so bloody bang. Check this:

My blood type is no negative, and I'm positive that I'm too deep
—Sexodus

You use new keys to type old deeds
Set up by old needs what world peace
—Karmageddon

My sights are set in higher times
And my eyes can see in 3D
Make it bright and I see 360
I can get you, but you can't get me
—Sexodus

Why did I tell you about my latest favourite artist though? Because it all comes down to this:

Make good art. Husband runs off with a politician? Make good art. Leg crushed and then eaten by mutated boa constrictor? Make good art. IRS on your trail? Make good art. Cat exploded? Make good art. Somebody on the internet thinks what you do is stupid or evil or it's all been done before? Make good art. Probably things will work out somehow, and eventually time will take the sting away, but that doesn't matter. Do what only you do best. Make good art
—Neil Gaiman

This is what makes me feel alive. My art.

And I know it will keep you afloat as well. You can write.

You've got a good taste and I know it's killer. Keep loving and keep writing, Nafisa.

Um, love, I guess,
Kiaan

◆

I looked up M.I.A. immediately, fell in love with her music, replaced Lily Allen with her as my lesbian fantasy and got down to writing my reply:

They can say whatever
Imma do whatever
No pain is forever
Yup, you know this
—Hard, Rihanna

Yeah, I know this. But being aware of these lyrics doesn't mean I'm dealing with my shit any better. I'll tell you what, all your theory and knowledge of life goes for a spin when death comes for a bout. Take my word, each one of us will be knocked out. No one can survive the hit.

What if I'm not an artist, eh? How are you so sure I'm one?

I've got a flurry of questions for you to answer. Oh yes, I did watch Mathangi's videos and she indeed is a sick one. I'm in love with her. Man, I'd give my arm to have a figure like hers and be half as creative as that.

Blaze a blaze galang a lang a langlang
Purple haze galang a lang a langlang

Back to my questions then. How will two introverts fall for each other? I'm ruling out virtual mediums – the internet doesn't exist, now what? Both of them are perhaps travelling in the same bus, their eyes firmly rooted in the book, oblivious of the world around them and wondering how love will knock on their door. Nobody makes a move; they're either too shy or scared. I'm not worried about their love stories coming into existence. I'm interested as to how they shall start.

In hindsight though, I'm glad you wrote about unrequited love. Every glossy and flossy novel sets up a love story to die for, but what if it never took off? That movie with the skinny guy who sang the madly viral song rhyming with 'Cola berry bee' came close though. Brilliant actor but. I toh loved him in the movie.

Ever heard of our notorious music composer whose name rhymes with 'Rhythm'? You could not have possibly ignored the streak of hit songs he's delivered over his career, over and over again. Yet his chartbusters are mostly stolen/copied/inspired. And the guy's poor luck, I tell you, when the music was for once original and beautiful, the movie turned out to be a collection of copied shenanigans. So the million dollar question is – who gets the credit for the chartbuster? 'Cause many times, I felt the copied ones by Rhythm were far superior in terms of music production than the original one. Unethical? Perhaps, but he did eventually better the art, right?

And last but not the least, I need to learn to survive the beast called 'night'. Stars don't keep me company anymore and I'm quite scared of sitting alone on the terrace now, afraid that I might be bombarded with mumma's memories.

Shaam dhale toh subah na aaye,
Raat hi raat chale

—Chupke se, Gulzar sahab

Whatever gets you through the night, it's alright, says apna John Lennon. How to figure out my 'whatever', Kiaan?

Love,
Nafisa

◆

To be honest, nights weren't so terrible with mumma's diary to accompany me. But the period between lying down and falling asleep still tried haunting me. So, if the painter had something for me, I was all ears. I kept wondering though as to why he was so confident of my artistic abilities. And with that query, I was off.

17

It was our usual sneaking out of college, diary. I didn't know that word, you guessed it right. Ghazal told me. She said, "You're not bunking college anymore. You're sneaking out. Bunking sounds wild, what you're up to is elegant. It's charming. Go, sneak out, meet him and make another happy memory."

So I sneaked out, didn't bunk. He was waiting on the terrace, sunlight and shadows taking turns to touch his body. His cheekbones rose, eyes got narrow and he blinked that insanely cute blink, slooowly, acknowledging me.

"Aaishapath, I love how he blinks slooowly, for you," Ghazal had mentioned.

"Yeah, it's cute."

"You don't just call it cute, lady. You attach an adverb to it. It's insanely cute."

I smiled, looked up and thanked whichever god/goddess had decided to send him to me. But, I couldn't admit this to him, diary. Because a love marriage was impossible for me. And falling in love, out of question. I had no other option but to hold back my feelings. I had to try pushing him away, diary.

I sat down next to him, wondering how to start the conversation. He lay there like he belonged with nature, at ease, in silence.

"See, I know where this is going. Based on my observations, you're going to or have already fallen for me. But I can't reciprocate, okay? I can't. And you seem so beautiful, I can't hurt you either. I... I... I can't live with the guilt of having hurt someone like you. So, if this is where we're headed to, it's better that we end it right now. We can't go on."

He took a deep breath, exhaled and looked away at nothing really, just looked away.

"I don't want to lose you," he said.

"Hmm?"

"That's the plain truth. I don't want to lose you."

I didn't know what to say. So I pursed my lips further and waited for him to speak again.

He turned his face, locked eyes with me and continued, "Yes, you're right. I have fallen for you, hopelessly so, it seems. Because you're beautiful. No, not that face of yours, the whole world notices that, I'm no exception. I have fallen for the Tamanna you've managed to hide inside, locked away somewhere.

"Love is about giving, Tamanna. I'll never ask you to reciprocate. But I'll wait, I'll wait, hoping that the magic kicks in. That you feel the butterflies as well. That your hands shake nervously, like mine do right now. The happy fear that your heart might pop out beating that fast. But then, you either feel it or you don't. I do and you don't, right now. So, I'll wait. But don't rob me of my right to love you."

"What if I never feel it?" I asked him.

"Well, it never hurts to have loved someone."

I took a deep breath, exhaled and looked away at nothing really, just looked away.

◆

Things were certainly moving fast, huh? I mean, an entry ago, mumma had just met him. And man, did he sound smitten or what! Well, that was not much of a shocker. How was mumma pulled in though? Umm, artists often shower their muses with that kind of adulation. For me, a muse has always been an object of destruction. The one who destroys you and yet transforms your soul into a gorgeous mess. Did he indeed feel for mumma or was she just a muse? Man, where was my papa?

18

I'm really angry, diary. Baba has locked me in this room. I'm also quite hungry. But it doesn't look like he'll unlock the room soon. Not tonight at least. I think we both deserve it.

So, this is what happened today. I had spent another wonderful afternoon with Jai. We discussed the architecture of Pune's buildings today. We both know nothing about the architecture they teach in colleges. But that is what I like about him. He turns boring things into objects worth observing. And then ends our walk with a trademark quote, as if he plans the entire conversation beforehand.

He said, "Look at all these wooden buildings and their balconies. What if an earthquake strikes us right now? I can bet these structures will be the first ones to collapse. But look at the building beside it. It's taller, looks stronger, more efficient and has a lift in there as well, but it's not beautiful. This wooden one however, look at it – the slanting roofs made of kawelu, elegant breathing balconies and windows with tinted glasses, what sets it apart?"

I just kept looking at him and the building, then the building and him.

"Don't worry, it was rhetorical. I wasn't expecting an answer," he laughed and continued, "What sets the wooden building apart is

its vulnerability. All of that beauty shall be shattered by the slightest tremor. And that which can't be destroyed is perhaps the most efficient, but not beautiful. That concrete building beside is advanced and safer yet fails to touch my heart. Because it won't fall. It's not vulnerable. A rose is vulnerable, at your mercy entirely; watching you intently whether you decide to pluck and kill it or admire and move on. It has given you the freedom to choose life or death for itself. Isn't it the peak of vulnerability?"

I was about to say yes, when he stopped me, "Rhetorical baba, it was rhetorical."

And he smiled his perfect smile.

He is beautiful, isn't he, diary? See, I have learned to ask rhetorical questions. Ha ha.

Imagine how happy I was after that walk with him. I returned home to hear the news that made me this angry. Baba had gone and arranged my marriage with a guy named Kailash. Arranged my marriage, diary! And he told me this news as if... as if... it was no more important than the rising prices of Aaloo and Daal he had mentioned before. Oh yes, diary. He mentioned the price rise and my marriage in the same sentence. I just stood there frozen, looking at him and aai, then aai and him.

I wanted to run away and cry. Scream and shout and cry actually. Six months from now, I am supposed to marry this guy with an uncle's name – Kailash. I walked straight to my room and put on the walkman. I didn't realize when side A's songs ended while I kept crying and cursing my parents for doing this to me. I switched the cassette to side B, pressed play again and continued crying and cursing. I was really really angry, diary.

I took the keys of baba's bike and drove it to Katraj highway. Before getting there, I also bought a bottle of kerosene and a matchbox. Then I set his beloved bike on fire. How could baba arrange my marriage without even asking me once! He deserved it. I kept looking at the orange fire against the black sky while Aashiqui's songs played on my walkman.

I took a rickshaw to return home. He was reading the newspaper, when I told him, "Kerosene's price has also gone up and I burnt your bike."

He didn't notice my statement at first, but then it struck him. He walked out to check on his bike and asked me repeatedly – did you, did you? First in disbelief, then in horror and finally he looked as angry as I was. And I told him, "This is how you feel when you lose something you love."

I was thinking of Jai, diary. Have I started loving him?

He was about to slap me, when aai held his hand. Baba grabbed my arm and locked me in this room then. I knew that the bike was dearest to him and yet I didn't feel guilty. He's cursing me right now as I'm writing, diary.

But he has burnt all my hopes and I have burnt his bike to ashes. We are even, I think.

◆

My god! Oh my god! Mumma burnt naanu's bike, wow! So she wasn't just an elegant graceful lady then. A storm in salwar, how's that? I had no idea that mumma was so fierce. That was some revenge but. I was already feeling bad for papa. He wasn't really in for a treat. Jai, that poet guy though. I could see what pulled mumma in. His words were indeed mesmerizing. And I'm sure he was delivering them with élan on their walks. Mumma's sudden outburst wasn't so sudden perhaps. Her hatred for arranged marriage and infatuation for Jai had reacted to create the deadly explosion. Oh wait, she burnt the bike on Katraj highway. But a lonely highway meant no night-crawling and a morning walk was out of syllabus. So I just prayed that the bike chassis decomposed in peace and then dozed off, feeling proud that my mumma was a bad-ass. Such wow, much love.

19

I was asked to meet Kailash today, diary. I haven't seen people meeting their partners before the eventual marriage day after the interview day. So, it was quite a bold request to make. I had no idea what to say to him. Well, we did meet and things are no different.

Uh… diary, he's really really boring and a silent kind of person. He doesn't talk much, you know. And whenever he did, it was about his boring job and office complaints. I was hoping that he would make it less awkward for us, but he made things only worse.

Opposites attract, they say and there's a reason they say so, diary, isn't it? Jai creates that balance when we are together. He talks and I listen. But how can we connect when both people won't speak and only silence talks?

He didn't even come to pick me up. I was to meet him on JM Road's Sambhaji Park. So I took my walkman and boarded a PMT bus. I like the clicking sound the conductor makes. You know diary, we Indians are great at making things simple and efficient. A rope and a bell, that's all conductors and drivers use to communicate. Click click ting ting. I wonder if we'll still be using them twenty years from now.

The window seat is my favourite. It somehow always puts you in a thinking mode. And Pune's weather is like that caring mother who might scold you in the morning, but who comes back with all her love when she and the evening both cool down. It always gets pleasant as the dark approaches. Always. I want to be a person like this. All other emotions can vary, but the constant factor should be love. At the end of the day, come back with it. With the pleasant love. Nature does teach you a lot, all the more when you sit on the window seat.

So philosopher-cum-nature-lover me got off the bus and walked towards the park gate. I had seen a photo of Kailash, but he wasn't exactly a handsome man and I hated his mooch. Uh, about mooch, I'm not sure if this is right, but how can I find the English word for a Hindi/ Marathi word? I'll have to ask Ghazal. In fact, I don't like a man with a mooch. A man should be like Amitabh as in Agneepath or Rahul Roy from Aashiqui, clean shaven and tip top.

He was already waiting for me. I waved to him, took off my walkman and put it in my handbag. He didn't wave back. Guess why, diary. He was holding ice-golas in both his hands and they were already melting. Why didn't he buy only one? I'm still wondering. He could have asked me when I came whether I wanted one.

Anyway, he was wearing black bell-bottom pants and a loose plain white shirt. He is quite tall and his haircut is pretty simple, too simple actually. What we call champu baal. Oiled and neatly parted. A green gola in one hand and a kala khatta in the other one, both melting. All of it was quite cute and I had forgotten for a minute that I was bloody angry about this arranged marriage. But then, I looked at his mooch and it brought back that feeling of uh, gust… something. Ghazal had told me this word, um, is… gust… disgust, yes, finally.

He did compliment me though, saying that the white salwar looked beautiful and that we looked kind of similar with my waist-long braided hair and black eyes making the black and white combination. Well, I had gone without any kohl so that I looked my worst but he still complimented me. So, he was lying, of course. Being polite just to marry me and keep a good impression. I didn't want to say anything then.

"What are your hobbies?"

"Hmm," I said.

"No, your hobbies?"

"Hmm, ha ha."

He had to ask for a third time when I realized I had to answer this one and couldn't just hmm and laugh it out. He was telling me about his job or boss or something, don't really remember. But once he was done with his ice gola, we just walked in silence in the park.

He shook my hand before I got on the bus. My neck was permanently hanging down. I had hardly made any eye-contact with him. Anyway, I grabbed a window seat then, put my walkman on and became the philosopher-cum-nature-lover again.

How am I going to marry this guy, diary? Shall I run away? Uh, alone or with Jai?

◆

Hey mumma, papa was cute, okay? Cuter than your poet guy, okay? With that frame of mind, mumma would have dismissed *saakshaat moochless* Amitabh as well. So, I won't blame papa. She had really thought of eloping or was it just a bad joke? How did papa bounce back though? Hmm. Things were getting really really interesting.

20

I'm gonna swing from the chandelier, from the chandelier,
I'm gonna live like tomorrow doesn't exist, like it doesn't exist,
I'm gonna fly like a bird through the night, feel my tears as they dry,
I'm gonna swing from the chandelier, from the chandelier

—Chandelier, Sia

If freedom was a person, she would sing like Sia and dance like Maddie. Really would. I haven't heard a better singer. Her voice is earth-shattering. Yes, a volcano erupts and touches the moon. That's how I felt when my speakers puked magic. It's the most aesthetically pleasing party-lyrics song you'll ever hear in your life. Take my word for that.

Now, if someone created a remix for this song and somehow managed to better the best, how would I react? Wait, I just said best, didn't I? How can I tag a song as the best one in its genre? For art is subjective. You might rate the remix higher. But you can only steal when there's something to be stolen. What if the original masterpiece didn't exist? So, for you, the Indian music director seems to click, but there might be a Turkish/Korean/Mexican/World citizen who might be cursing him for ruining their favorite original versions. You say he elevated the songs, they might beg to differ. For art is subjective.

But then, good artists copy, great artists steal. I shall pass no judgments here. I have provided my share of inputs and you can choose to agree or disagree. I'm a sponge. I don't judge. I simply keep absorbing. The entire universe is senseless. So, attach the interpretation that makes you feel satisfied. Art is simply art. It just exists. You can either glorify it or vilify it or go fuck yourself. Art won't care.

A love story of an introvert couple without the internet, huh? Well, I don't really have a philosophically beautiful or smart-ass reply for that. So I'll pose another question.

Fate or free will – which one is governing us? If you ask me, free will is a scam. Every large chunk of your life is already fated – the kind of person you shall become, the person you shall end up with, how you shall die – it's all decided already. Free will is limited to the smaller chunks of life like when you fall asleep, decide to poop or hold it in a while longer, to lift your ass or bunk college for the day, et al. So, internet or no internet, if a love story is meant to transpire, it shall. No force can prevent it. It can start in silent libraries, boring college corridors, tasteless canteens, exciting bookstores, thrilling music concerts, forgotten letters or the mysterious virtual space. If it is meant to be, it shall find a way to happen. And you'll finally have a story for your grandchildren.

The night is coming closer. How to survive one then, hai na? Simple is beautiful. So I'll blurt out the truth. I can't possibly console you here. Cry yourself to sleep. Simple as that. Or the controversial option – ooh, aah, masturbate. Nothing else can induce sleep like it. Choose wisely. There's no single cure for this.

Honestly, I can't write to you with the motive of healing. You would hate me even more for that. I can just hope that my letters somehow soothe the pain and help the numbness fade away with each word. Perhaps, one of my letters shall also try making you smile.

Oh oh, by the way, is sketching a hobby that remained limited to the most ignored drawing period of your class?

Okay, whatever your answer may be, come to see the revolution at COEP college, 8 a.m. this Sunday.

Love,

Kiaan

◆

This fucker had seamlessly moved from Sia's song to inspired art to just art to philosophical debate to night endurance lessons. And as much as I hate to admit, I was convinced by his arguments. This guy, I tell you, such an ass! I actually pined for his letters. Always had a way with words, this painter.

Of course, I was gonna go. How could I not meet the one who was healing me without trying to heal me? Kiaan. Bloody talented ass!

21

I experienced my first kiss, diary! First kiss, yes! A lip kiss! Oh god, my hands are still shaking and I can barely hold the pen. I didn't mean to, but the setting just made us kiss. I'm in Goa right now. Surprised, right? Well, it took an entire month to convince my parents for a weekend in Goa. Ghazal helped me with all her charm.

I'll come back to the kiss in a while. Let me tell you about our trip first. So, the four of us actually left for the trip, while my parents were shown the girls-only fleet of our class. This mad mad lady Ghazal requested, ordered and even begged our classmates to show up for a fake trip. Four of us, who? Jai, me, Ghazal and her lover Noor. I saw him for the first time when we dropped off our fake tour-mates a couple of kilometres later and switched to a taxi from a bus. An evil evil plot carried out with great planning. And of course, you know the mastermind behind all this.

Back to Noor then. Jai sat with the driver, while Noor and I occupied window seats. Ghazal told me about him only about a month ago. The trip and her lover were mentioned together. I wanted every little detail about the story and she promised to fill my bedtime with those stories on the trip. Is it something common with all the mysteriously elegant boys – their oh so graceful slight smile, the glow in their eyes when they look at you and the love with which they observe the world. His language was refined and elegant like an Urdu poet. Even his casual conversation sounded like poetry. Within an hour, I had no doubt that he was perfect for her. Only an artist could mesmerize her like that. The most beautiful muse deserves the most beautiful artist.

Did you notice the words being written twice? Mad mad, evil evil, so so, hmm, diary? Well, Ghazal suggested this.

"If you want to emphasize something, repeat the words. It sounds cute. And it also provides you the control over your readers. I know, the diary is only for you, but if you happen to read it say ten years later, those word pairs should make for a great reading experience. It's a win-win."

I was really excited about exploring Goa. I wanted to visit every beach we could. And so we did. I got to wear jeans finally. But I would still prefer salwars. Ghazal and Noor spent the last day in their room, joining us only for dinner. Today, all four of us went out though. I loved the feeling of my naked feet on the sand, with the water taking turns to meet me, leave me, meet me, leave me. Didn't love the salty water though. I mean, yeah, that's how the sea is, but no salty water in my mouth, ears, eyes, hair. No, thank you. I hated the taste. And god knows what really goes in my mouth. I saw people spitting in the sea, perhaps they even urinate in it. Who knows? So, I wasn't going into the waters, for sure. I got busy with sand castles, writing names that were erased regularly, digging up the mud and watching it get filled with water.

Oh yeah, we also visited Chapora fort. And what a lovely sight it was, diary, I swear to you! I could not differentiate between the sky and the sea from the top. They were so blue and beautiful. I hated the climb and kept cursing Jai for the idea to visit a fort, but it was worth it. I was beginning to see what drives this philosopher sort of people – waves, sky, flowers, sunlight – basically nature. They suddenly become far more romantic when closer to nature. That's what the yellow of the sun, green of the grass, blue of the sky and red of the rose does to them.

Back to the kiss? Jai asked me for a walk and we roamed on the moonlit roads. With each step, he came a little closer to me. Then he touched my palm with his and I understood his desire, locking our palms. He had never revealed this aspect of his personality. It was surprising that he could go for a walk and not say a word. We just walked and returned to the hotel, holding hands all the while. As I was walking to my room, he called my name. I stood at the door as he walked towards me, staring into my eyes all the while. I could feel his breath on my face, he was standing that close. But I wasn't uncomfortable. I let him. We just stood, breathing. He then both his palms on my cheeks, tilted his face, closed his eyes and leaned in. I didn't know how to react. So I just stood, breathing. And then our slightly wet lips met. He had stopped breathing. He was kissing me, the grip of his lips tightening over mine with each passing second. I closed my eyes as well. A few seconds later, he pulled back for a breath, looked at me with his slight slight smile and kissed me again. I closed my eyes and stopped breathing with him this time. I felt my hands just hanging uselessly, so I rested them on his back. He breathed in while still kissing and I followed him. The magic of the kiss faded after a couple of minutes though. It became really wet and sloppy and weird noises. The first touch was electric however. The first touch. A lip on a lip.

I told all this to Ghazal first and decided to write it down for you, diary. Because I want to remember this night for years to come. I think, I'm in love with Jai. He didn't say anything after the kiss, but I could just sense it in his walk, palms and eyes tonight. Or maybe the moonlight on my window is trying to fool me. Marriage is only two months away, diary.

◆

Ohkaaay! This mumma-Jai thing was getting quite serious. And I wasn't having a good feeling about it. This relationship wasn't throwing off good vibes onto me. Two months before her wedding and mumma escaped for a weekend in Goa with him! Damn! Where does papa win her over? Or did he never… no no no no no no no. Please please please, god, make this poet guy falter somewhere. Wearing jeans was such a luxury for mumma, huh? Quite a Goa trip though, I must say. Unlike mine. So so unlike mine.

It reminded me of Amar. I hadn't texted or called him since a couple of months and neither had he bothered to make a move. Not that I was complaining. I wasn't exactly missing his company. Umm, was I being unfair to him? I made a run for the bathroom that night to check on my tattoo '*Amar prem*'. It had almost faded out of existence.

22

Sleeping at 6 a.m. was routine. But getting up at the same time, uhmm, not my cup of tea. If the smartphone failed me, I had a human alarm clock as the permanent backup. Too bad I had lost that luxury of dependence on the most reliable human species on earth – mothers. I often wonder if I would make such countless sacrifices for my babies. Anyway, I had read that if you instruct your mind to wake up at a specific time and think of it before dozing off, your body shall wake you up. I didn't trust my genetically lazy body, so I adopted the tried and tested method. Drink water abundantly before crashing and your bladder shall take care of the rest. Okay, enough of my early morning woes, let me reach COEP.

Now the thing is, COEP had its campus on either ends of the road. And I wasn't sure where the revolution was to occur. Damn that bloody talented painter who could write! Yes, his invitation had created a sense of mystery, but I was soon cursing him for the inconvenience. My genetically lazy legs were being made to walk in a people-barren campus on an early morning. Talk of horror!

After a round of aimless cuss words accompanied by heavy panting, I appeared at the other end. I saw a clueless girl looking at the building, examining it and scratching her head. I walked further to notice an aged man, sitting cozily in a tiny cloth chair, employing pencil to write a graphical poem on paper. And then the sketchers kept popping up, in innocent corners of the campus. Few had chosen pillars to draw, few were relishing the elegant architecture of the COEP building, while the rest of them hoarded the serene steps leading to the river that reminded of a countryside locale. Pencils, charcoal, brushes, poster colors, water colors, pilot pens, pens were making love to the paper and creating magic. I could see why Kiaan had termed it a revolution. No words uttered, yet an artistic upheaval was taking place. And nobody could have guessed. They were robbing the brilliance of COEP campus in broad daylight. And nobody was complaining.

How was I to locate Kiaan though? I had no idea how he or his sketches looked. So I just kept strolling, stalking people's drawings and admiring them with a wide open mouth. After an hour, everyone gathered around the banyan tree to showcase their finished work. There were ten odd guys for me to analyze. Damn his knack for theatricality! I turned on my detective mode and started looking for clues. I observed all the sketches on display and all bore their creator's signature. That's it. How simple was that! I just had to wait till, okay wait, there was no signature that even faintly resembled a 'Kiaan'.

That's when someone tapped on my shoulder and said, "Signature, huh? You underestimate my intelligence, Nafisa."

◆

I turned around to see the man himself. Salt and pepper hair, pepper beard, black eyes, charming smile, a loose kurta, an absolutely dirty jeans marred/painted by poster color patches that looked absolutely artistic and freaking awesome, and a pair of flip-flops marked the end of my visual judgment.

"Hey, mister painter who can write, huh?" I said.

And he bowed and said, "Pleasure is all mine. A walk?"

I had walked enough for a month already, but then he smiled and uh, no, it didn't make me forget the sprain in my legs, so I requested, "Shall we sit on the stairs? We'll walk next Sunday perhaps."

The river screamed silence and kept waiting for us to begin the conversation. Honestly, I was still busy admiring his absolutely dirty jeans.

"It began with justified rage, your first letter, I mean. I'll also write you one – an angry letter with unjustified rage. Things that make me angry. Consider that letter as the reply to your first one. Unrequited love wasn't a fitting reply, I suppose. Anyway, how are you holding up these days?"

I just shrugged my shoulders. We both knew the answer. The pain was never going to subside, so I showed him the facade – a smile.

His eyes reflected the sunshine back and asked, "What drives the art in an artist? Is it love or hate?"

"Uh, it's 10 a.m. dude."

"Yeah, so?"

"Isn't it too intense a question for, uh, I don't know, *vada paav* time?"

"That's how I roll," he said, shrugging his shoulders.

I cursed him again for the intellectual inconvenience and began pondering.

"Well, isn't the answer obvious?"

"Obvious truths often require the hardest hardships."

Okay, I must admit, that was a brilliant quote to quote at vada paav time. So I decided not to complain anymore.

"Ahan, go on."

"Whenever I was pissed off, I started painting. I usually waited to get furious and only then started working on my sketches. Whatever was wrong, I wanted to make right. I went for calm walks alone to make myself angry. I thought of all the things that infuriated me. That got me going. I had discovered my magical potion for creating art. They say, you need to endure a huge volume of your work before it actually begins to satisfy your own taste. And I agree with them. It wasn't great work, but I was improving. I could see it. That was when it struck me – what was driving me?"

He paused for a dramatic effect. I gave him his moment. Why? Because salt and pepper hair, man!

"Was it love or hate? What was the driving force? Did it even matter that I decode the reason?"

"I guess, it would make you self-conscious. So, uh, don't."

"That was rhetoric."

God, I felt so stupid then.

I cursed him for making me feel dumb and recovered, "Aha, go on."

"No, I'm done. That's all I had to say. You know the answer anyway, don't you?"

"Well, yeah, love it is. All great art emerges from true love and passion."

Okay, I must admit, my quote wasn't too bad as well for a *kaandaa poha* after vada paav time.

Kiaan acknowledged my quote with a smile and said, "See you next Sunday then? Shaniwarwada. Same time."

"But I can't sketch."

"Bring pen and paper with you. That's it. Write a poem, stir up a novel's plot, draw a tree, whatever. Just come, okay?"

"Yeah, I guess."

He got up to bid me adieu, when I asked him, "You sure, you aren't a writer? I mean, a full-fledged writer. Don't say no, because your letters suggest otherwise."

"My first love is a paintbrush, not a pen. Having said that, I do see a full-fledged writer in you though."

"Me? Seriously?"

"Don't say no, because your letters suggest otherwise. Ciao."

23

And as promised, the painter did send across a letter.

RANTIEST RANT

You wanna know the things I'm angry about, huh? You really wanna know, huh? Okay, take this.

I'm on my bicycle and I see a bike come over. The helmet is hanging, tied to the bar above tail-lamp while the rider is busy flirting with the accelerator. I wish that he gets hit by a truck or something while crossing the intersection. And the helmet should fall off right beside his beheaded head. Yes, they deserve that.

I'm on my bicycle and I see another bike come over. No helmets this time, neither on the head nor on the tail-lamp bar. Oh, a pair of earphones/headphones adorning those ears though. Yeah, music is absolutely essential when you're driving a bike, duh! I swear to god, the day such a biker gets involved in an accident and doesn't die from it, I'll go and beat that fucktard to death. I keep praying for such a day.

I'm not on my bicycle finally and observing children walking around. Most of them are carrying their father's phone or a big-ass tablet. Go play, you moron! Eat some dirt, learn to curse and beat up few guys or get beaten up. Touch that dew and walk on that lovely grass with your naked feet. But no, they want to abuse the naked screens with their naked fingers. That's their childhood now – memories of a stupid screen.

Sex. Yeah, sex. Taboo for the generation before us. The deadliest sin. Fucking overrated, this sex and the virginity. Elders created the hoopla around pre-marital sex, equating it with guilt, while our peers have made a joke of it. Sex is a norm and condoms are new eclairs. They waited too long to get a taste of it, while our generation can't wait too long. While we were still busy giggling at the pictures of genitals in our biology textbooks, kids these days are already busy with practical sessions. And here I am, stuck somewhere in between, busy doing a social commentary and waiting for my license to have sex – arranged marriage. Yeah, talk about sexually frustrated Indians!

I see myself in the mirror and go bonkers. A French beard seems an elusive entity for my hormones. I've tried razors, trimmers, scissors, prayers and nothing works. Trust me. Bloody nothing works! My moustache and goatee are meant to never meet. I watch all those perfectly trimmed beards being sported by almost every man in existence except me and I feel like running over all those beards with lawn mowers. I endure intense rage on a daily basis. The reason is the facial hair that refuses to grow in a straight line from my upper lip to the chin.

And last but certainly not the least, in fact, I saved the best for the last. Friendzone. Yeah, you heard that right. That's my superpower. I enter it with the consistency of South Africa failing at ICC events. Always, yes. Man, I have ended up convincing girls that they're better off single than entering a relationship. That bad! Maakikirkiri!

I love you like a perfect friend.

What the fuck does a perfect friend mean?

I like you, but I don't want to spoil our friendship.

You can make love to a stranger from an arranged marriage, but a relationship with a trusted friend, no sir, no.

I don't feel those vibes for you. You're a great friend though.

Yeah, great friend, my ass. Achaar daalu main great friend ka?

Oh, there are no good guys anymore, you know. I want a guy like you for a relationship.

Well then, choose me, for fuck's sake. I'm a guy like me!

You're such a great guy, you know. I would certainly date you, but...

But you're doomed to stay in the friendzone forever. And I can't help it. Go fuck yourself.

I have figured out the formula for the incoming friendzone missile. It's a sentence loaded with fake compliments for you, ending with the phrase 'but I'm sorry', followed by the evergreen consolation that there's a non-existent great girl waiting for you who you shall meet never, err, I mean, soon.

It's cent percent true and I certify it with absolute certainty that good guys get heaven and bad boys get girls. It's a sad sad deadlock actually. A good girl is drawn to a bad boy, gets her heart broken, goes on to break the hearts of good guys, turning them into bad boys eventually, who start the hunt for a good girl's heart.

Phew! Fuck my life!

And fuck this shit,

Kiaan

◆

I was seriously weighing the thought whether Kiaan was a psychopath under the guise of an engineer-painter. Damn, his letter felt like a note from an Indian version of *American Psycho.* I prayed that I don't do anything silly to invite his wrath upon me and dozed off. I had skipped the diary that night. Motherfucker's letter had spooked me enough to induce sleep. Before dozing off though, a thought had flashed and vanished – mumma and I were living inverted lives perhaps. I was busy writing and reading letters, while she was the one having walk dates.

24

So with a pen and paper, I arrived at the Shaniwarwada fort. It was a serene morning and the pleasant chilly wind almost managed to make me jog, almost. There was an elevated platform, sorta stage, right before the entrance that allowed you to see and be seen 360 degree. So I picked the most innocent corner of the premises and began scanning the place for something within my puny ability to draw. Okay, so lemme see what we had – a majestic door, airy windows, overwhelming walls, gorgeous balcony and a ferocious statue of Bajirao. And no points for guessing, I chose the Banyan tree at the farthest end of the place.

I began with the trunk and then drew connected semi-circles around it. I guess, I was done. God, I was so embarrassed to look at it. The drawing skills of the three-year-old-me and twenty-one-year-old-me hardly differed. I crumpled the paper and threw it away. While I was at it, Kiaan had already spotted me and was at a school-bus distance when he waved.

"Hey, what you up to?" he asked.

I showed him the blank paper and said, "Thinking about my next book."

"Wow. Really?"

I cursed myself for not saying a poem. But I had to continue the lie.

"Yeah. Fiction, I guess."

"That sounds interesting! What's the plot?"

"Uh, haven't yet figured out a plot."

"I see. You keep pondering. I'll start."

He chose to sketch a section of the wall with those large stones. I wondered what was so unique about a section of stones when one had an entire fort to capture. Didn't ask him though.

"What would you like to read? Or let me rephrase, if you think I'm a capable full-fledged writer, what would you want me to write?"

He completed the rough layout by drawing a set of crooked and perfectly straight vertical and horizontal lines.

Then he looked up and said, "Hmm, let me see. Okay, there are two kind of writers. Those who can cook up a brilliant plot with intriguing characters and setting. Such a plot, even if not executed with finesse, can hook a reader. Won't blow them away of course, but hook them, yes. Then, there are those who just happen to write interesting content. Such people need a workable plot and that's enough for them to sprinkle magic on paper."

"And I am?"

"Latter one, obviously. Your vibrancy comes across whenever I read you. And suddenly ordinary things seem to gain an air of importance. Ordinary becomes extraordinary. And I guess, that's the key to writing great fiction. To put magic in the mundane."

"Umm, thanks?"

And he splashed across the rough layout a grey water colour patch. I would have colored it with a sketch-pen and minded my boundaries. I noticed he was wearing the same pair of jeans, dirtier this time and thus all the more beautiful. But, I guess, that's the brilliance of a true artist – they don't mind boundaries, they break them. Or simply work as if the boundaries don't exist. He let the patch dry down a bit, before opting for a black pilot pen.

He started adorning the paper wall with little black dots and it had begun to come into existence.

"What will be the plot though?" I asked him.

"What sort of genre you like?"

"I'm not really sure. I haven't read any of the classics, nor am a fan of heavy-duty literary works. I read normal people's normal content. Light-hearted with a pinch of wisdom and absolutely raw. That's more like my thing. Also, if it can make you laugh and cry at the same time, that would be a great bonus."

He kept dotting and nodding as I was explaining, and the wall was about to start breathing soon.

"Your own life would make for a good book then. No need to do any research, nothing. Just write whatever you have been through and I'm sure it will come out well."

"Really? Are you serious? My life? What's so special about my life? It's ordi…"

"Exactly. It is ordinary. Whose is not? But can you find the magic in there, that's the question."

"Why do you keep repeating the word 'magic'?"

"Uh, I like the word?"

He finished the dotting and the wall was finally complete. Gosh, I got several goosebumps. It felt unreal that it came into existence while we discussed my lie.

"Now, that's magic."

He smiled at me and signed it – a curvy K, followed by a pointed dotted I, loopy A's and finished by a wavy N.

"Well, I hope my letter shall find a place in your book."

"Oh, that? My god, that was quite a rant. Weird, crazy and insane as well, if I may add. Let's discuss it next Sunday?"

"Sure. Fergusson College. Same time. Think of a title for your book then."

"Magic?"

"Nah, something catchier, something catchier..."

And I left with an actual desire for writing a book. Well, it all started with a lie. So don't blame me if this doesn't turn out well for you.

25

Kailash had called me to the Sambhaji Park. And I arrived with my walkman, using them for as long as I could before he started talking. I don't know what was about that place and his obsession with melting ice-golas. I didn't even want to ask him. Why? Well, I didn't care. It's a punishment, no, diary? To get to know someone not because you want to, but are made to.

He kept asking questions like I was appearing for an interview.

"What are your hobbies?"

"What makes you happy?"

"Tell me more about you. What kind of movies you like?"

I kept my answers as short as possible, diary. I behaved quite rudely, to be honest. But that's what I aimed for. I wanted to come across as the worst possible future housewife.

"Nothing really. But I hate cooking the most."

"Nothing really, oh no, no, wait, um, I like fancy jewelry and expensive saaris."

He pointed out that I always wore a salwar. I argued back, diary.

"Well, I would love to wear expensive saaris then. Something I want."

"I don't like going out for movies. There are so many people in a

theatre. And I feel very weird. They laugh together, chew together and talk while the movie runs. In fact, I don't like going out at all. I like staying at home."

He replied, "That's nice. Even I prefer to remain at home."

Aaichyagaavaat, I thought. I had described my hatred with such conviction that it was useless to change my statement then. So I let that be.

A walk with Jai is different, diary. With Kailash, it felt like a great effort. I wanted to sit down and ordered him that we do. He agreed instantly. Ha, I won't be impressed so easily. He's very, uh, obedient, diary. And I have no way to find out if it's his original behaviour or just for the sake of showing off. Who knows, he might rape me on the night of our marriage. Such nice guys might turn out to be complete psychos.

A couple was sitting in front of us with their crying baby. Kailash just kept staring at the baby and smiled. I felt sooooo awkward then. I thought the father would come and scold him. But soon the baby started staring back at him. Kailash started clapping and making faces for the baby. Well, it was cute, diary, but since I had planned to be really rude to him, my face had the expression as if he was trying to kidnap the baby.

I looked at the baby and got lost in my own thoughts. A baby will come out of me in the coming years, I thought. A shiver ran down my body as I imagined the pain. And all the relatives gathering around me to think of the baby's name, everybody giggling and me wanting to kill them all. I mean, I wanted to be a mother, but, uh, somehow escape the pregnancy? Stupid, I know. But I have the right to wish.

Kailash broke my wishful thoughts, saying, "Uh, Tamanna?"

"Haan?" I said.

"I want to tell you something. Uh, I'm not the richest guy you'll meet, not the most handsome either; I'm not even great at conversation skills, not exactly an interesting person. I think, you must have figured that out by now. I am boring, to be honest. I am just another ordinary

guy with a job who is of marriageable age. Uh, we are going to spend our lives together. And it's never easy. I have seen my parents quarrel. So, it's better that you have the truth right now. I have nothing else to offer to you, except love."

I saw the sincerity in his eyes as he spoke the words, but I still wasn't ready to accept it.

"What if I love someone else?" I asked him.

"I want you to be happy, with or without me."

His eyes were still sincere and it felt like he had given me the truth. But I couldn't accept it from him. I got up and ran away. Yes, diary. I ran and ran fast for the bus stop. Was that his original behaviour or a plan to fool me till the marriage? How was I going to figure out, diary?

◆

Way to go, papa. He was making it happen. And that finishing line – nothing else to offer to you, except love? How good was that! It takes a brave man to deal with such a resistant lady. Papa, however, acted honestly and gently. Mumma was being real rude to papa. Not cool. Was that the finishing move though? Because mumma still sounded in love with that Jai.

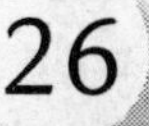

26

Kiaan's words had rekindled my love for reading. I couldn't remember a single day when I had picked up a book since with Amar. Nevertheless, I had chosen the pirated copy of the book wherein both the lovers are cancer-afflicted, fall in love (obviously!) and then one of them dies. My god, that book is absolutely brimming with hauntingly beautiful quotes. The title has stars in it, all the more reason that I loved the book. And I loved the dark humor throughout the book. I couldn't stop crying while reading the letter in the climax. But it made me smile as well. Maybe we all deserve a love story like that. That was the perfect point of reference to write my own book. The title, the title though. How was I going to figure out my title?

I was basking in the pleasure of having finished the brilliant book and having bought it after intense bargaining that had saved me a hundred bucks. What a life! That's when a surprise text arrived from Amar: *At your college gate. Meet me outside. Let's go for a ride. :-**

Okay, honestly I wasn't in the mood for a ride. I wanted some me time. To just lie down and relive the book again. And that, my fellow readers would know, is supposed to be a solitary activity. But I couldn't say no to my babe. It had been a couple of months that I last saw him. It was all Kiaan. And Amar wasn't even texting me, perhaps respecting my need to recover from the trauma. So I couldn't blame him for a surprise visit. Um, he must have been missing me. Had *I* missed him though?

I grabbed a pullover and made a run for him in my shorts. Figuratively, of course, I didn't really run for him. I don't run for *me*, man. Oh wait, one more for my college's bloody large campus: Your college so small that if Usain Bolt made a run, he would cover the campus under five seconds. But I guess, thank god for that? I reached the gate pretty soon. Damn right, I love my *tingusa* campus.

Amar put his cheek forward, expecting a kiss on the cheeks, but I wasn't really in the mood. So I just became the pillion rider and tapped on his shoulder. He took us to the peaceful lanes of Koregaon Park. But we had to endure the endless honking traffic before reaching the rewarding silent lanes. He parked and we walked.

"How are you holding up? I was missing you badly today."

"It's okay, *baba*. You don't need a reason to come meet me."

"I still don't know what to talk. But I need you around me. And I don't want to invade your space as well. But I miss you. I was wondering you might call me one of these days to talk a bit, but you didn't. Texting was anyway not going on. So I thought you needed some space. I waited and I waited but I couldn't, today."

"It's okay, honey."

And he had given me the answer. I hadn't missed him. It was not a conscious choice to not have called him, rather it never crossed my mind to give him a call. Was I *so* invested in Kiaan? Because I did need company. And I had chosen Kiaan's letters and the sketching-less morning meetings. Was it only 'bang bang, thank you' thing for me? Well, we never did 'bang bang' per se, but you got my point, right? Kiaan never said that. He always had something to tell me, something to teach me. He never tried to soothe me and yet had such a calming influence. It was as if he had read a manual on how to deal with a soul that had encountered a brutal death. Amar, though, remained clueless. It was a viva question from the reference books for him and he had no idea what it even meant. He tried stammering but local publication could do only so much. Long story short, was Kiaan invading the space once Amar owned in my heart? Kiaan, that mad carefree painter who rode a bicycle all around the city, had not even asked for my number yet. And yet he was the one I wished was walking with me. Yeah, you heard that right, by the way, a bicycle, whatever the distance may be. He was a true-blue old school guy.

I had asked him for a ride back to my hostel and he had pointed at his bicycle and enacted a puncture. Very funny, fucker! I had mouthed.

"Why do you ride a bicycle, dude?"

"*O eco-friendly, nature ke rakshak, main bhi hoon nature.*"

"*Sadda haq, aithe rakh*, huh?"

"Bicycles are romantic and sensible."

"And slower than the equally romantic bike rides and senseless for a ten kilometre drive."

"Well, that's how I roll."

I recalled the incident and chuckled.

"Hmm? You saw something funny?" Amar asked.

"No, nothing. Listen, can we go back? I am kinda sleepy. I just finished reading a book today."

"Okay, sure."

I made up an excuse. I wasn't sleepy. And Amar didn't even ask me what book it was or how did I like it, nothing.

Something collapsed within me that night. I don't know if *I* made the jump or was pushed off the edge. I didn't utter a word on our way back. I wasn't even hugging him the way *Jungli Jawani* hugged Jordan. It was as if I was being possessed by that painter's soul, kilometre by kilometre. I got off the bike and stood facing him at the college gate. He looked at me and I stared at the ground. I looked up to see that he was moving in for a lip kiss. I was startled and thus stepped back. He looked at me and I stared at the ground. I looked up to see that he was going, going, and gone.

27

I'm sad and disappointed, diary. It's the kind of day when you are too tired to be angry. I'm just exhausted from fighting this marriage. We attended a wedding today and it only added to my insecurity. I'm scared, diary.

Anyway, who do you think is the most patient man? It's not a monk. No. I don't agree. A bus driver, facing the burning sunlight and dealing with stupid drivers, is. Those are the conditions that test your patience and tolerance. A monk sitting under a tree in a calm forest has nothing to get angry about. It's as good as it gets. No offence meant to Gautam Buddha, haan. Just a random thought.

Aai had finally convinced me to attend the wedding. I was in no mood to go. In fact, I am in no mood to attend mine either. It's like an examination, diary, you know. And all guests are the judges. You need to be dressed perfectly, walk perfectly, smile perfectly, cry perfectly, oh oh, in fact, cry like a bitch (Ghazal taught me that, obviously!).

"Oh, I'm telling you, Tammy, you need to cry like a bitch in your bidaai. Or be prepared for a lifetime of allegations and shaming like: 'You weren't sad to leave your parents, huh?', 'You don't love your parents at all!', 'Didn't cry at all that girl, what a shameless creature!'. Well, fuck this shit, I say. But, it's better to comply than to rebel. A moment of

convenience might lead to forty years of stupid arguments. Just keep me close for your bidaai, I'll pinch you hard on the elbow and bring you to tears. Don't you worry, babe. I got your back."

I still wonder where she learns those phrases and words from. Haven't heard from her since a week as well. She's not attending college. I'll wait for another week and visit her if needed. Anyway, back to the wedding I attended. I had resolved to keep a count of all the wedding waste. I'll start listing then.

1. As soon as we entered, we were handed a bunch of flowers and a small bag of rice.

We are supposed to throw those at the bride and bridegroom. But guess who we throw them at? The person sitting couple rows ahead of us. So except the first two rows, nobody gets to actually throw them at the people getting married. It's like Holi with flowers and rice. A shower and shampoo session is absolutely necessary when back home. Complete waste.

2. I absolutely hate firecrackers, diary. Simply hate them. Really really hate them. I mean, it has to be the most idiotic invention of mankind. We spend money to hear a loud noise and see a few glittering lights. And that noise makes us and animals almost deaf. So essentially, we pay to make ourselves deaf. Also, noise pollution. A lot of it. I shall never understand the pleasure of hearing a thousand-cracker-series (popularly called as ladi) burst. It's just unending noise, really. Real pleasure would be to see the shaadi ka mandap being burnt down by one of the crackers used for the celebrations. That would be a great sight. Am I sounding too evil, diary?

3. Food. Oh. My. God. To be honest, we can feed another army of wedding guests from the leftover food. And people. Oh, the bloody people! Nobody wants to see you marry. Nobody, diary. They judge a wedding by only one thing – the food. I swear, as soon as the last word of 'Shubh mangal savdhaan' was uttered, people got up to run for the plates. I had to hide behind aai to avoid being run over by the rushing hungry audience.

And all of it is going to happen yet again in a month. What do I do, diary? I'll have to smile endlessly for all the guests and wedding album. And makeup. My biggest enemy. Except for kohl and eyeliner, I have never needed or used anything else. The bride today had a kilo-bhar of foundation and lipstick on her face. Yikes! (Ghazal taught me that, obviously!)

Only a month, diary. Shall I confess my love for Jai? Do I really love him, diary? I'm so confused right now. What exactly is love? And Kailash has asked me to meet him for one last time next week. He is a nice guy, but, uh, I don't know, diary. I'll go meet Jai tomorrow and see how it goes. If nobody else, he can certainly tell me about real love.

◆

God, I was so scared to turn the page and read the next entry. What if Jai confessed that he loved her back? Only a month away from the wedding and papa was still struggling. I spent the night lying wide awake, for the suspense was too much to bear. But I had to endure the night to get my answers, just like mumma.

28

"What is love, Jai?" I asked him first thing.

No hello, no nothing, diary.

"I'm not exactly in the mood to talk about love. Can we just walk? I have something important to say."

"No, I want to know, Jai. This is extremely important for me. And I don't have much time."

"Is it more important than my struggle for a job? Really?"

"Already applying for jobs, are you?"

"Not commerce jobs of course. I want to establish myself as a poet or lyrics writer. I'm trying to look for industry contacts who can help me give a break. I can't work in a 9 to 5 job. That's not me."

"I'm getting married in a month, Jai."

"Oh..."

Jai remained intense and thought for a while. I thought, that fact had made him realize something. But it wasn't so, diary.

"I can't think of marriage right now. I need to create an identity for me. This is the time to sleep hungry if needed, but keep pushing. It's my only dream. I want to write as much as I can and gain recognition. It won't be easy. So I don't want any commitment to interfere with my ambition. I can't look after a girl right now. It's not the time for marriage."

I was really hurt, diary. He didn't mean to, but I was extremely hurt. It was as if someone had sucked out oxygen from my body. I had to stop myself from crying. I thought, he would fight for me against the world, if needed. I was really hurt, diary.

"I wish the best for you, Jai. You would make a great poet. That I'm sure of. Nobody can stop real talent. You'll make a great poet…"

"Thank you, Tamanna. And you'll make a good wife, I'm sure."

I wanted to ask him, did he never really love me, not even for a moment? And what about our walks and conversations? But I couldn't bear to hear the truth. So I buried the questions within my heart.

He said, "Love. Poets and philosophers, since the beginning of time, are trying to figure out and define what love is. But there's no single definition. We all feel it in our own unique way. I think, it's the constant undercurrent. Something that shall never fade, no matter how hard you try. It shall occupy a permanent place in your heart. Attraction is like the high of an alcohol, it's the best thing ever while it stays. But then, love has to take over when things settle down, love has to fight for the couple when they are the worst versions of themselves. It's when the entire world refuses to believe in you, but your partner sees something and resolves to fight the world's word. It's when you teach your partner to see themselves in a different light, when they can't. Their happiness becomes your first priority. And both the partners strive to become a better human being, with each passing day, learning something worthwhile from each other. It's when you know someone is intensely flawed and immensely imperfect, but they have dared to expose their real self to you and have given you the power to hurt them. You become the vulnerable rose that can be plucked off and that's when the love blossoms. You give in to your partner and are assured of your personality more than ever before. And yet with all that power, you pray every day that your partner shall never break your heart and crush it to powder. Well, love comes with its own pleasure and pain. You can't only choose one. It will be intense as a blazing fire and safe as a safety warehouse. Nobody else can make you smile like they can. Nobody's touch will be as electric. Nobody's words more soothing. And even if you were dead inside, you'd wish to live another day just to see them and hear them talk and embrace you and your soul. If it fades, it's not love. Love is the permanent stab in your heart."

I couldn't hold it in anymore. I had to leave and find a place to cry alone. Was I not beautiful enough for him, intellectual enough for him? I wanted to ask him all this, diary. But I simply could not. I wanted him to realize his dream. I couldn't be selfish. If I really felt for him, I would want the best for him, right? I wanted to see him happy, more than anything in this world. I just listened today, diary. I could not confess my feelings to him. I just listened, even when I had left with only one thing on my mind – to talk to him. I always listened to him, diary. I could never reply.

When I was waiting for the bus, he said, "Don't take my word, Tamanna. Think for yourself. Your questions deserve your answers, not mine. Only you can define your love, not me. What is your definition? Once you figure that out, you shall know what love really is."

I got on the bus and got off at the next stop. And I cried and I cried, diary. Jai would never know how strongly I have felt for him. It's of no use telling him now. What I'm worried about is, will I love again? Or have I even loved Jai? Was Jai my definition of love? How will I get my answers, diary? How?

◆

Mumma was crying and I was so happy. I didn't like that poet guy anyway. He was giving out such bad vibes. I knew something was gonna give, uh, let's say, I was rather praying for it. So, Jai was out of the picture, but mumma still felt for him. Quite strongly, in fact. Did she really love him though? And was she going to marry papa with those feelings still alive? Do something, papa. We ain't got much time.

29

I spent last night crying all alone. I just could not stop. It was the lowest and saddest I had ever felt. Also, I didn't have Ghazal to talk to. I had to face it all alone.

I had to meet Kailash today, though. I was looking horrible, diary. I had not oiled and combed my hair, left them loose for the first time, eyes were all red and looked really really tired. My nose was still a little red as well and cheeks felt heavy as if the water had seeped in and added weight. I just dressed in a sky blue salwar, put on my black kolhapuri chappals and left. No eyeliner, no kohl – nothing.

He was waiting for me as usual, with the ice-gola in his hands, melting away drop by drop. He always bought two and always bought them before I even arrived.

"Hi, you look diff…erent today," he said.

Well observed, I said within.

"Yeah," I said.

"You look more beautiful today, in fact."

Thanks for the biggest lie ever, I said within.

"Umm, thanks?"

"You want to marry me na, Tamanna?"

His tone had suddenly shifted from happy to serious.

What choice do I have, I said within.

"Hmm," I said.

"Because if there is anything you would like to tell me, I'm here to listen to it. Anything. I won't mind. But this is the last chance to raise an objection. If you don't like me, tell it now. And I won't mind. I promise, I won't. It's the biggest decision of your life, which is kind of forced on you. So if we marry, I'll hope that you have nothing to hide from me and will start with a clean slate. I just want you to be happy. If this marriage won't, let me know and I shall leave. No questions asked. But this is the last chance."

I don't care if it's you or someone else. I just hate the concept of an arranged marriage. Nobody can make me happy, when I'm so angry inside. How does it matter, huh? You or someone else, what difference does it make? It's all the same. I hate arranged marriages, it's like gambling with your life, literally. Now that we are brought together by our fates, I'll just go ahead and marry you. But I don't know if I'll ever give my soul to you. I don't know if I'll ever love you, I said within.

"There's nothing to tell you. We are marrying. I just had a bad day yesterday. Something that hurt me. Uh, but it's okay. Don't worry," I said.

A baaraat was passing by, with the brass band playing the tune of all the hit dance songs from movies. I love to dance, diary. But I was so sad inside and felt so helpless that I just sighed and decided to watch them pass by. Also, even if I was fine inside, would I dance in front of Kailash? I'm not that comfortable with him yet. Would he be fine with me, dancing in a baaraat with no care in the world?

But then, the most unexpected thing happened, diary. Kailash went ahead and joined the baaraatis, dancing miserably. I mean, I haven't seen a dancer worse than him. Actually, he didn't even dance, diary. His body just moved from one awkward position to another. Oh god, it was so funny. I mean, just imagine him moving around awkwardly, with a melting ice-gola in a hand, moustache on the face, champu hairstyle, a silly smile and flying bell-bottom trousers that was dancing in its own way.

I was laughing within. But I smiled faintly for him. I could not laugh in front of him, diary. I just couldn't. But I was laughing a lot within. Few people around me were laughing at him though.

'Look at that stupid man. What a loser!'

'Why doesn't he mind his age? And this guy will marry a girl someday or already has! Poor girl that. I pity his wife already.'

'Saala chutiyaa!'

I felt like punching all those people. Go mind your own business, I wanted to shout to them. As I was staring at those people angrily, Kailash walked up to me, all sweaty and breathing heavily. And I suddenly felt so embarrassed. All those people who were passing comments were staring at me and laughing, diary. I just wanted to vanish. I didn't want to be seen with him.

"Those people were calling you a stupid loser," I told Kailash, pointing at those men.

"But I saw you smile."

"Uh, so?"

"Then how does it matter?"

And he just smiled at me, looking really really happy, with his eyes wider than ever, while sweat kept dripping from his eyebrows. I couldn't control it, diary. I smiled back at him.

◆

Oh papa, my lovely lovely papa, my heart just melted there. And mumma was also beginning to see you for what you were. But she had just begun. Was that enough for her to wipe out the feelings for Jai? Because she didn't sound happy with the marriage. It sounded more of a helpless surrender. Did she ever manage to love papa? A woman's heart conceals secrets like no other. And I wonder what she had kept hidden in there during her married life.

30

I was beginning to develop a plot in my head for the book. I knew where I was going to start it. That night of the fateful breakup. Writing it won't be a big deal, I had thought. It would be a fictional work and I'd get to experiment with the concentration of truth in it. Pretty easy, haa! I was walking over to Kiaan. Another Sunday morning, another awe-inspiring venue with ethereal architecture. Fergusson College. The salt part of his hair kept shining brilliantly as his hand moved in violently gracious motion. It was a pencil sketch. And he had chosen the entire building this time, not just a part of the wall.

"Dreaming bigger, aiming higher, huh?"

And he looked up at me, a hair strand obstructing his eye-view, raising both his eyebrows at once to convey a 'What's up?' and continued sketching with that lovely smile.

"What choice does an artist have?"

"What about us ordinary souls then?"

"Love someone and be a good person. That would be really kind."

"And what about the artists? Just create good art?"

"What's with you this morning, huh? Good art, artists, ordinary souls? It's not even vada paav time."

"Well, you got me thinking about that book. And I'm going to write it. I'll write it, mister painter."

"Why don't you have a pen and paper with you?"

"I just wanted to see you. I won't write or sketch anyway."

It was something intense – what I felt for Kiaan. It was as if I had to match up to him somehow, in all his brilliance and nonchalance. The intensity of his smiling eyes, sketching fingers, and raging words had captivated me, hypnotized me. I was pulled in, he didn't mean to. And he had been such a gentle soul. Full of precise love, measured love, somehow bounded and yet felt limitless.

"Desires don't complete a book."

Kiaan broke my train of thought and my continuous stare switching from his hands to eyes to hair to lips to that jeans.

"What does it take to finish a book? Or any piece of art for that matter?"

"Passion, devotion, love for it..."

"Yeah, exactly. I knew it."

"...are not enough. That's what gets you started. But talent can only take you so far. It takes immense patience and discipline. It won't always come flowing outta you, so you'll have to fight it out, write bad shit, edit it and rewrite. Perseverance is the key."

"Oh, I see."

"And people."

"What about them?"

"Fuck the people."

"What?! Why?"

"Nobody deserves your time. Allocate all of it to your art. People are not worth it."

"Books are not life, you know. There's a real life waiting to be lived with real people, real emotions and real problems."

"I would rather live in the bubble of mine. If I had to choose between my dream and people, I would gladly choose the former.

People disappoint you, dreams don't. Your dream won't wake up one day and say it doesn't love you anymore."

"Says who?"

"Says Lady Gaga."

I pondered for a while and asked him, "What about love then?"

"What about it?"

"If you'll never expose yourself, be the real you, let your guard down for a while, how shall someone make a way to your soul? To love at all is to be vulnerable."

"Says who?"

"Says C.S. Lewis."

"Lover for me would be the one who has all the answers to my questions. Rather, only her answers shall make sense to me. Someone I can respect and love and adore and perhaps fear at the same time."

"Wow! Ain't that a lot to ask for?"

"I won't compromise. There are so many ordinary things in our life, love should not be one of them. I've set my bar quite high. Someone shall either cross it or will have to explode the fucking bar. And until I find someone like that, it's my dream and me. Nobody interferes with my ambition."

Was I good enough for him? Was I his definition of extraordinary love? I had thought of confessing that I feel for him, but simply couldn't. I'm quite an irreverent soul, but his presence and words had somehow inspired a sense of respect for him and part fear and part hatred. Maybe I was yet another people for him. But I had to know, I had to.

"Kiaan?" I said.

His face seemed so perfect and his lips just soft enough.

I cupped his face and kissed him. And I kissed him and kissed him some more. When I got up, his lap was shaking and he could barely hold the pencil again.

I said to him before leaving, "You are going to be a great painter and artist, Kiaan. Perhaps not the best lover, but a great artist, for sure. And I hope that makes you happy. Because, not all people disappoint. Some rare ones have a magical ability to make you feel happy. And I dearly wish that you spot one soon, darling. Even the best ones needed a muse. Nobody has made it alone. That kind of loathing might make you blind to someone who already cares for you and perhaps would love to be with you. I'll see you soon, sweetheart. And yeah, I'll write you a beautiful book."

I lauded myself for that finishing touch before leaving. If I had a storm brewing inside for him, he deserved to have one too. The storm inside that questioned both of us – was it something special?

The Climax

I hate the world. I hate people and the stupid society. I hate marriages and the need to marry. I want to scream and shout and break… no, no…destroy things. I want to kill all of them, diary. I WANT TO KILL THEM NOW!

This can't be true, diary. It can't be. How can her own brother… no, it can't be. I'm so scared, diary.

It is the seventh day since Ghazal had eloped with Noor. She had promised she would call me. And I just kept waiting.

You won't believe what I saw in today's front page news. Ghazal and Noor had been killed a week ago, on the same day they tried to elope. Her brother and father were already aware of her plans and waited to catch her red-handed. To kill both of them. They put him on fire first. Imagine the horror in her eyes, diary. To see your love being burnt alive. And then they cut her up. That's like dying a couple of deaths. Those men who are apparently her father and brother! They shouldn't be sent to jail. Hand them over to me. I'LL KILL THEM RIGHT NOW!

What do I do, diary? What do I do in a world without her? My beautiful crazy gorgeous brilliant chaotic Ghazal. I'm just crying since I read that news report. Just crying and feeling helpless. I hate this world. I'm just filled with this anger right now.

"Love is never a sin; not listening to your heart is. Better choose that life your heart craves. Compromising is not living a life, Tamanna. Don't live forty years of a mediocre marriage. I would rather choose a single night of staring at the stars with him. I can't pretend to be alive, being dead within. Nobody deserves that. Not you, not your partner. That's like spoiling two lives instead of one. I choose to be bold and face the consequences. My love shall stand by me."

This was what she told me before she left. And I happen to remember it word by word. I'll tell this to my children as well. That's how your love is supposed to be. Beautiful crazy gorgeous brilliant chaotic. Just like Ghazal.

"Ghazal might be a form of song, Tamanna, but I feel I'm the dance of divinity. And so are you. In fact, we all are. We're a soul roaming around in a chunk of meat, floating in this space made of stardust. The meat is bound to die someday, but there's nothing to fear. For nobody can kill your soul."

I miss her, diary. I really do. Maybe it's because of the time we're living in that she died. I can bet that people won't be killing lovers for their false pride and ego in say twenty years from now. Why twenty, I'll say ten. Stupid stupid stupid world.

You know what, I can't write anymore. I just can't. You started because of her and it's only fair that you end with her, diary. I'm sorry. Bye.

◆

What?! Oh my god, what? I flipped the pages frantically, but there was nothing written after that. The diary had indeed died with Ghazal. Poor girl Ghazal. I felt so sorry for her and mumma. How did we end up corrupting the concept of love with castes and religions? Horrifying and absolutely shocking! I couldn't sleep. I needed answers; I was restless; the night haunted me, man. Coming morning was a weekend and I was planning to head for home. Papa *had* to know about mumma's diary. Since I couldn't sleep, I decided to make amends with my forgotten allies – the terrace, moon, and stars. No stars adorned the sky that night though.

I ordered myself to calm down and compile the list of questions I wanted to ask papa.

Oh god, was she happy with her marriage?

Did papa treat her well all these years?

What happened to Jai?

Did she still love Jai while being married?

It was as if someone had torn off the last few pages of a thriller. For a reader, there's not a terror greater than that. Man, I was so going home first thing in the morning.

I'll just cut to the chase. Papa was busy with his newspaper and tea when I arrived. I took out the diary and sat facing him. I knocked on the newspaper.

"Yes?"

"Papa, I want to talk to you. Okay, I'll just apologize in advance because my questions won't exactly be pleasant. I'm sorry, but I need to know a few things."

"*Bolo beta*, it's okay."

"Did you know about this?" I asked him, pushing forward mumma's diary.

"Magic, huh? You writing something? Oh, 1991…"

He flipped through the pages and realized it was mumma's handwriting. He kept it back on the table. His facial expression changed from a smile to a stern one, and asked, "What do you need to know?"

"Did mumma love you? Like, really loved you or married you just because she was made to?"

No answer from him. He kept staring at the floor. And I started shooting the compilation of my questions and allegations.

"Did you know that mumma was writing a diary? Almost half of it is dedicated to a guy called Jai. Do you know what happened to him? She has barely mentioned you in there and hated the arranged marriage thing. You wanted to let her be happy, right? With you or without you? Was mumma happy? Tell me, papa! I need to know."

Papa got up and went to his room. I was sorta fuming by then. Why didn't he answer? Was he guilty because I had offered him the truth? I could literally hear myself breathing. I wasn't a panda anymore, more of a dragon who wanted to set everything on fire.

Papa returned with a sealed letter, tears in his eyes.

"I haven't loved any other woman in my life and I never will. Was Tamanna happy? I would like to think so. I wish she was here to answer that. She was the one who had a choice to make and chose me. I never forced it on her. That letter has all the reasons why she made this choice. She handed me that letter on the night of our marriage, wanted me to read it. But I never opened it. Because it didn't matter. I just promised to keep her happy, no matter what. I have loved your mumma with all I had. Don't you ever…"

His crying had intensified. He turned, walked and locked himself in the bedroom. I felt immensely guilty. I was in tears as well, one of them falling on the sealed envelope. So it all came down to the letter. I would have all my answers. The climax. I opened the seal carefully and began reading:

Dilemma. Ghazal taught me that word to describe the turmoil of my heart. It would have been easier to make the choice if she was here. So, dilemma. When you need to opt for one out of the available options. Well, I had humans to choose from. And my life was at stake.

Is it possible to love two people at the same time? Maybe, yes. It's safe to say so because I've had the moment of the dilemma. Who was the other guy then? Jai. My classmate. He was a torch who put my aspirations on fire. I had never known how to live life. He taught me. He taught me to love nature, architecture, human emotions and my own life. He taught me to fly within the cage. Yes, I was trapped in the cage of an arranged marriage, but nobody had stopped me from flying. He gave me the wings. He pushed me off the edge. I was hypnotized by his words and philosophy. He had unlocked the key to my heart – he made me feel alive. It's a lot for someone who's dead inside. Dead dreams and dead expectations. Jai helped me dream again, see myself in a new light. But did I love him?

Ghazal had told me once that you can never love someone out of pity. Being with Jai made me realize that you can't love someone out of fear as well. I thought I loved Jai. Absolutely. Unmistakably. It felt like love. But when I asked my heart, it whispered back the answer to me. They say, our heart knows. It somehow always does. It was admiration disguised as love. I respected him. I looked up to him as a student looks at their teacher. I had kissed him when we were in Goa. That night, he had leaned in for the kiss. And I had let him. It was a submission to his aura. I wasn't the real me around him. I couldn't be.

I hate the concept of an arranged marriage. I think, you must have figured that out by now. And I hated my parents for tying our fates together without my permission. I burnt baba's bike to ashes the day he told me about you. How would you like it if your future rested in the hands of ignorant parents? It's always the girl who gets married and loses her lover. And a guy always loses his lover to an arranged marriage. I haven't seen a girl lose her guy to a marriage ever. Holes are drilled in both the hearts and it becomes a story to be hidden forever in our incomplete diaries.

Whenever we met, I have been really really rude to you. And you always welcomed it. You never raised your voice. I gave you enough reasons to do it, but you never did. Still, I was not ready to trust you. So I always doubted your behavior. There was no way for me to know.

I thought of eloping with Jai, but never could do it. Why? Because he wanted a perfect human being, rather a perfect copy of his expectations. I was a shapeless piece of clay when I met him and he turned me into a beautiful piece of art. But I couldn't remain a perfect piece of art all my life. I couldn't stick to his principles all my life. He rarely made me smile, you know. Whenever with him, I had a constant expression of awe on my face. I never adored him however. I walked with him, but was falling for you all this while.

Why did I choose you? Because I'm still imperfect and I get angry, I shout at people, I dance with the radio and I cook tasteless daal. But I know you'd accept me with all my flaws and still love me. Jai won't. He needs someone who can stand up to him, challenge him intellectually and live a life on his principles. He taught me to love, but I always had the fear of letting him down. And when you are conscious of that feeling, there can be no love. Fear of failing can only bring out respect and obedience and submission, never love.

With you, I realized, I could be me. The real me. And that acceptance is wherein lies true love. You knew you'll have to make a few compromises and adjust to my behavior, but you welcomed it. You welcomed it with sincerity and honesty. You welcomed it with a smile and melting ice-golas. And I'm glad. I'm glad that I chose you. I'm glad that I decided to marry you. No regrets.

I couldn't have told you all these reasons face to face. So I decided to write it down in a letter and hand it over to you. Thank you, Kailash. For whatever you have been to me. For the darling that you are. For offering me nothing, but your love.

I love you.

Yours always,

Tamanna

◆

I banged on the bedroom door and screamed, "I love you too, papa. Mumma made the right choice. I'm so sorry."

Salty tears flirted with my tongue as my hands trembled for the phone. The darling had no dilemma anymore.

I called him up and confessed my love, "I'm not the richest girl you'll meet, nor the prettiest one. I'm imperfect, I get angry, I shout at people, I dance with the radio and I can't cook. But my sweetheart, I know one thing for sure. I love you. Yes, I love you. I have nothing else to offer to you, but my love. Will that do?"

And he replied, "Till I die."

Epilogue

The night is here and the lights are off and your memory invades my senses. I want to hear your words, see those eyes of yours again and fall in love over and over. I'll hug you so tight, I would never let you go. I'm glad that I make you happy. I'm blessed to have you, awesomesauce you. And we'll work on it, not just wish, that our souls remain attached to each other. I just love you as long as your eyebrows and as deep as your eyes. You're a gift to me. I'm at peace to have you here. I won't let you go, sweetheart. You belong with me. You are mine. And I'm yours.

Nafisa

PS: Don't believe the guy on the cover who claims to have written this book.

Acknowledgements

My mother, Karuna – for making all the sacrifices and being the tireless selfless mother. My late father, Jairaj – I miss you.

Nayan, Sachin, Nilesh, Amey, Pankaj, Milind, Darshan, Aarti – for providing critical inputs that helped build the plot.

Gaurav, Sumit, Vishwas, Prashant, Ashish, Akshay, Rahul, Pratik, Pujan, Poorvi, Tanya – for being the kind of friends one dearly wishes for.

Shweta Mirani – for being the heart and soul of Nafisa.

Shikha, Pratibha, Shreya, Neethi – for being such exceptional ladies and all the conversations that are reflected in the personalities and dialogues of the characters.

The entire team at Srishti Publishers for making this book happen.

For Kavyal.

I love you.